1-800-CHRISTMAS

JOSIE RIVIERA

INTRODUCTION

To keep up on newly released ebooks, paperbacks, Large Print Paperbacks, audiobooks, as well as exclusive sales, sign up for Josie's Newsletter today.

As a thank you, I'll send you a Free PDF … The Beauty Of …

Josie's Newsletter

Did you know that according to a Yale University study, people who read books live longer?

This book is dedicated to all my wonderful readers who have supported me every inch of the way.
THANK YOU!

Amazon Review by J. Shields:

"I really enjoyed this book. It was a first for me by Josie but it will definitely not be my last. I loved the story line. It takes us back to high school and blends that interest into today. There was one little twist but I am not going to tell you as I don't want to give it away. That woman didn't deserve a dime but Kieran made the right choice to keep her out of their lives. It runs you through some emotions as Desiree and her sister Candee grew up with just each other and a slew of crappy foster homes. It is great, though, what they have done with their lives.

It is a small town book, add in some house flippers, a carpenter wanna be chef and a lawyer who doesn't want to give her heart away. If you are looking for a cute read this is the book for you. Just be prepared for the emotions. Highly recommend anything by this author!"

Amazon Review by Marie B.:

"Desiree Contando has trouble trusting after dealing with drunken parents and being shuffled from one awful foster care home to another. She grew up thinking football star and popular student Keiran O'Malley had it so easy and despite having a crush on him that he would never want anything to do with her.

She never dreamed that he would end up living in the attic apartment in her fixer upper while doing carpentry work on it. I loved reading all the wonderful recipes that Keiran cooked up. I would definitely eat at his pub. This was a sweet holiday romance with plenty of humor and yummy foods."

Amazon Review by Liz:
"Ms. Riviera had me hooked right at the start.
I did not want to put it down."

PRAISE AND AWARDS

USA TODAY bestselling author

CHAPTER 1

Desiree Contando had gained weight. Not a lot, although the extra ten pounds on her five-foot-four-inch frame were enough to make her favorite linen skirt fit snugly around her waist. When she was stressed, she ate pumpkin pie. Lately, she'd eaten a lot of pumpkin pie, and she had blamed it on Thanksgiving.

However, it was more than the delicious turkey dinner her sister, Candee, had served. The cause of Desiree's stress was the rundown Queen-Anne style home she'd purchased that morning.

"Your house is beautiful." Candee's voice came from behind her. "Now we both live on Thompson Lane!"

Desiree swallowed hard. "Maybe my house will be beautiful in a thousand years."

She shouldn't have done this. She should have dashed out of the lawyer's office as soon as the closing papers had been handed over for her to sign.

"Mr. Dunworthy, the former owner, never got around to updating the home, and then Teddy didn't have time," Candee said. "Your house won't take long to restore. My dilapidated Victorian is proof that even the most ramshackle house can be renovated."

Teddy and Candee had met in Roses, North Carolina, when Teddy came from Miami searching for a house to flip. They'd married, and together with Teddy's nephew, Joseph, they'd moved into a sprawling Victorian. Teddy had been granted legal guardianship of Joseph a few months earlier.

Desiree pushed out a tight breath. "Your Victorian still needs tons of work."

"Thankfully, it has come a long way." Candee stepped to Desiree's side and flitted her a once-over. She carried a box of pumpkin muffins. "A housewarming token," she'd declared, with a promise of something better coming on Christmas Eve.

"You've accomplished so much this year," Desiree said.

"I'm following your example. Advocating justice for low-income families and children is a daunting task. Fortunately, you're a talented attorney."

"I'm just doing the best job I can."

"You're ensuring the poorest people receive fairness. I respect you." Candee's gaze wandered to the rambling house. "You have more than enough acreage on your property for horses."

"I'll leave horses to your animal expertise. And puppies."

Months earlier, Candee had adopted Kisses, a pregnant beagle, from the local animal shelter. Of the six puppies Kisses had birthed, only one remained, as Candee had sold the rest.

Candee's emerald eyes glowed. "Boomer is adorable—all black and white and tan. And he loves to eat."

"Are you planning to sell him?"

"He'd make a great companion for a special someone."

"I'm sure you'll find a forever home for him."

"I'm sure I will." Candee smirked. "Speaking of animals,

Teddy finished the stable for Joseph's horse therapy. He converted a large shed, and Joseph loves the Haflinger horse. I did my research and the horse is small, with a calm temperament."

"You're wonderful parents. I'm thrilled for all of you." Desiree stared at her house. It seemed to stare back, taunting her. She took a slight step and pressed her lips together. "I don't know if I can do this."

"Of course you can. You're experiencing buyer's remorse." Candee gave Desiree's hand a gentle squeeze. "Everyone panics after buying their first house. Remember, Teddy and I are only two doors away. If you need anything, text me. Better yet, flag me from your driveway."

"Please thank Teddy for selling the house to me at such a bargain price. I'd never have been able to find such a terrific value on my own." Desiree attempted animation, and knew she wavered.

"You have a successful job, and now a home to call your own." Candee kept her hand on Desiree's. "Look how far you've come."

"We," Desiree corrected, keeping her voice light. If she began reminiscing about their miserable childhood, she'd lose it. If she shared her thoughts, they'd both lose it.

The women had been shuffled to five different foster homes in their teens after the state had deemed their parents unfit. Drugs and drink were only part of the issue, as their parents had also struggled with mental health problems. They had died a short time after landing in jail.

Candee broke the somber mood with an encouraging beam. "Just think, you'll pay off the mortgage in thirty years."

"Thirty years." Desiree groaned. "It'll take me forever to find someone with the expertise to fix this house on my limited budget." She paused, willing herself to say her ex-boyfriend's name aloud. "Scott had promised to help."

Not physically, of course, because Scott never got his hands dirty. Nonetheless, he'd agreed to rent the dormer apartment in her attic. In addition, he'd referred his handyman cousin to tackle the house repairs at a reasonable cost.

Some boyfriend. Some *ex*. Desiree had counted on the rental income to help pay her mortgage, and a jack-of-all-trades guy to get the job done. Finally, she had her own house, but no one to share it with. No happily-ever-after.

"Scott is in the past. Forget him," Candee said. "What's worse than a guy who is only around during the good times?"

"I know. It's just . . ."

It was just that it seemed like years had passed since her and Scott's argument, although the breakup had occurred the previous evening when he'd accompanied her to the final walk-through of the house.

"Are you joking? This tumble-down nightmare is your new house?" he'd shouted.

"Well, if you had taken time out of your day before now to see it, you wouldn't be shocked," Desiree had replied. "The owner was elderly, and I told you the house needed a facelift."

"A facelift?" Scott had laughed. "Wow, Desiree. The house is a disaster. Is that your smooth-talking attorney jargon kicking into gear?"

"Are you ready to go inside?" Candee asked.

Desiree shifted and checked her shoulder bag for the house key.

Nope. She didn't have it.

"It's better Scott exited before you made a serious commitment to each other." Candee shuffled forward. "Besides, small-town life didn't fit his high-profile aspirations."

"True."

In Roses, life was slower, and people were friendly. A bandstand featured hometown entertainment. Tony's, the local pizzeria, had been there forever. Quaint and charming, the town hadn't given much thought to modernizing.

And now that Thanksgiving was over, the small town was transformed into a magical Christmas wonderland, a virtual postcard. Soon, snow would dust the pine tree branches and outlying mountaintops with a white sheen. Horse-drawn carriages circled the village green every weekend, and scents of gingerbread and cinnamon courtesy of local artisans filled the air. A holiday baking contest was held every year, and Desiree always entered her pistachio cake. She'd never won, although the twenty-five-dollar entry fee was donated to the local animal shelter.

Certainly, the happy Yuletide season and sense of community were reasons Desiree loved Roses and never wanted to leave.

A gust of icy air swept across the house's expansive front lawn, causing the oak tree branches to sway. The chilliness was a firm reminder that winter would soon secure a foothold on their Blue Ridge Mountain town. The wind was like a physical nudge, blowing across Desiree's thin navy suit jacket and bare legs.

She gripped the blue headband holding her thick blond hair in place.

She was out of luck. Her hair had blown into a mass of unmanageable waves.

Willing herself forward, Desiree stared at the various-shaped slate shingles on the roof necessitating repair, and the patterns of varicolored brick laying up the exterior walls. A century ago, the house had been designed to impress. Regardless, did anyone else use green, red, black, blue, and beige on one house?

She shouldered her red tote bag and matched Candee's steps.

This was a moment that Desiree had envisioned sharing with Scott. A life-changing threshold, embarking on their future together. They'd discuss her vision for the house, spend cozy winter evenings thumbing through decorating magazines, and wander paint stores discussing the perfect shade of dove white.

Velvet red ribbons and vibrant green garlands decorating the home's enormous rooms would celebrate Christmas in department-store style, and glittery white lights strung across the expansive front porch would create festive charm.

Now, all these special yet-to-be created memories would be done without Scott, because he was gone.

Her chest tightened, and she told herself to rein in her disappointment. Quietly to herself, she'd even hoped he'd pop the marriage question, bringing their dating arrangement to a happy-ending conclusion. She'd become Mrs. Scott Black, who lived in the beautiful Queen-Anne home on Thompson Lane.

Wow, had she ever been living in a fantasy world.

Between yesterday and today, the dream had disintegrated, and marriage was no longer in the cards. She was reaching thirty years old and every romantic relationship had resulted in a bad breakup. She was beginning to think she would forever be single and relegated to being addressed as Miss Desiree Contando.

Candee was staring at her, apparently wondering about Desiree's peculiar behavior, and why it was taking her so long to enter her new home.

"Desiree?" Candee tucked a strand of auburn hair beneath her faded baseball cap. "I know you're worried about taking on the house repairs, and I understand. When I mentioned to Teddy about your split with Scott, he made inquiries and found a carpenter for you. The guy's relocating here from Atlanta, Georgia. Apparently, Roses is his hometown. He told Teddy he'd like to give back to the community."

"Why would he leave Atlanta with the holidays a few weeks away?" Desiree asked. "Does his family live in the area?"

"Teddy didn't mention anything."

"And this guy's willing to start giving back by renovating my house?" With an overall sweep of her hands, Desiree gestured to the overgrown lawn, the neglected front porch, the weathered slate shingles on the steeply pitched roof.

"Yes. Teddy talked with him, and the guy will be arriving today."

"Does he know how much work my house demands?" Desiree challenged.

"You'll have to ask him yourself. He's reported to be talented and honest."

"Let's hope he's also cheap."

"He'll give you a good price." Candee firmly grasped Desiree's elbow, guiding her up the gravel driveway. "Teddy wanted to make amends for selling you this house when you clearly have reservations. He knows you're in a bind now with Scott gone."

Right. An understatement, to say the least.

Desiree changed her focus from her home's corner tower to Candee. "Who is this carpenter?"

"Keiran O'Malley."

Keiran O'Malley.

His name lodged in her throat. She had to fight down the feelings stirring within her.

"The O'Malleys owned O'Malley's Irish pub, which shut down many years ago," she managed to say.

The image of a tall, green-eyed guy with wavy dark hair came into Desiree's mind. He'd been on the high school football team, his broad chest and strong shoulders emphasized by his well-fitting jersey. He'd been a couple of years ahead of her, and had never given her a passing glance.

She'd glimpsed him at the homecoming game—the only one she and Candee had ever attended. When you lived in as many foster homes as they had, high school socializing was non-existent. Someone had pointed him out as the wealthiest kid in town. From what Desiree had heard, he sometimes helped his parents with their pub, key word being *sometimes*. Usually he was too busy escorting the current prom queen to country club dances, or driving around in his shiny new Ferrari after football practice.

After the game, she'd thought about talking with him, because her heart skipped a beat as she'd watched him. But, he'd been too engrossed in flirting shamelessly with a pretty cheerleader to notice Desiree.

Talk about a guy being off limits. In any event, they had run in completely different social circles. That is, if living in foster care counted as a circle.

"Teddy believes you can benefit from Keiran's carpentry skills," Candee said.

Panic rose inside Desiree. There would be a huge amount of work involved in transforming this house into her dream, and she remembered Keiran as seeming to be the opposite of ambitious.

Was it too late to sell her house back to Teddy and admit she'd made a mistake?

She pressed back her panic and concentrated on the second-story porch—the bracketed columns and neglected ornamental detail.

And the two words the house screamed: money pit.

She grimaced. "How does Teddy know Keiran?" she asked.

"Keiran remodeled a kitchen and bath in Georgia and

someone from Teddy's crew saw his work and recommended him."

Another gust of wind made the women shiver, and Candee jammed one hand into the pocket of her gray hoodie. "Earlier today, Teddy called Keiran and hired him for your project."

Desiree scowled. "Your husband did all this without asking me first?

"The guy's cheap, remember? He's coming back to his hometown and you'll be his—"

Desiree hesitated to finish the sentence. And then she did. "His first client."

"Exactly." Candee cheerfully ignored Desiree's apprehensive glance. "You want to host Christmas Eve dinner in your new house, correct? You can't do that until your kitchen is in working order."

"Regardless, I've never been known for my culinary skills. Except for my pistachio cake."

Candee laughed. "Um, even that's debatable."

The giggles came easier now, and Desiree's mind raced with trying to find a good reason to refuse Keiran's help before he arrived.

"I'd like to see his work. I have a certain design in mind, shabby chic, and I want it to be flawless," she said.

The laughter faded from Candee's face. "Flawlessness isn't the only thing that matters. Sometimes you take what you can get depending on your budget." She extracted Desiree's house key from her purse.

So that was where the key had gone. Desiree had forgotten she'd given it to Candee for safekeeping. Was this a sign she didn't really want the house?

Don't be ridiculous. If it was a sign of anything, it was that she was absentminded.

Candee lifted the key in the air. "Be content."

"Contentment and flawless should always be part of the same sentence."

"Not in our home-flipping world." Candee did a slow whirl, motioning toward the majestic trees, the worn picket fence, the trampled, overgrown bushes. A recent rain had soaked the lawn, and the grass was smeared with clumps of wet clippings. "Every house is a challenge and yours is no exception." She caught Desiree's hand. "C'mon. We've prolonged the inevitable long enough."

Sharing a chuckle, the women stepped onto the porch. Candee inserted the key into the lock, clicked the brass handle, and held the door open. "After you."

They stepped across a straw welcome mat, leaving footprints in the layer of dust on the aged parquet floor. Candee switched on the lights and offered a bright smile. "Oh, and there's one more thing about Keiran."

Desiree hesitated. "Only tell me if it's good."

"He planned on renting a place in town until he got on his feet," Candee said. "So Teddy recommended your attic apartment. He assumed you wouldn't mind if Keiran lived there for a while. The rent payment will help you with the mortgage."

A light fixture in the hallway swung precariously from an unsightly wire, and Desiree silently grumbled. "Is Keiran also an electrician?"

"Possibly, but he may not be licensed. I'm sure Teddy will know someone who is, though."

"Will a free room equal free labor?" Desiree waved off her sister's assurances. "And will his results be immediate? I want the house presentable by Christmas."

"C'mon, Desiree, don't be impatient. You're obliged to supply him with a salary and money for materials. Celebrate your good fortune because he dropped directly into your lap." Candee checked her watch. "Joseph's school bus will be coming soon. The school has early release because of a teacher planning seminar. I'll text you later."

With a nod signaling agreement, Desiree accepted the muffins and thanked her sister.

She took two paces into the foyer. A bone-deep weariness made her anxious, whereas Candee's enthusiasm was a source of inspiration.

Desiree drew on that inspiration. Taking a deep breath, she marched through the foyer and headed to the living room. The stained gold carpeting was peeling at the edges, and she bent to fold it back. Beneath the carpet were hardwood floors crying out for refinishing.

A large marble fireplace took up half the wall, its wide mantel solid oak. At Christmas, she imagined the mantel transformed, complete with sprigs of holly, miniature tealights and classic quilted stockings.

An unexpected downpour spilled across the bay window, and Desiree hoped that Candee had beaten the rain and reached her house without getting soaked.

She passed her fingers over the mantel, locating several candles and a box of matches, a reminder that Teddy had used the fireplace. He'd mentioned the HVAC unit wasn't operating, which meant no central heating or air conditioning.

The lights in the foyer blinked, then went out.

Already? Desiree massaged her temples. She hadn't been in her new home ten minutes.

Have faith, and everything will fall into place. Practical matters first. The encouraging words from her "forever family" foster mother came to mind.

Certainly, Desiree thought, she should hold fast to that wisdom.

First, deal with the electrical problem. And then the plumbing, then the . . .

The list went on and on.

Whereas now she had Keiran, the playboy turned carpenter who was on some kind of bizarre mission to help the community.

She went to the kitchen and placed the muffin box on the counter. Quickly, she captured her tote bag carrying overnight necessities, climbed the oak staircase to the master bedroom, and changed into an old pair of jeans and a flannel shirt. Although the light would soon fade, she'd begin the first afternoon in her new house by scrubbing the tiled floor.

Fun way to spend a Monday evening, she thought wryly. Fortunately, the plumbing was functional, and Teddy had kept a pail of cleaning supplies beneath the sink.

Although she had a love/hate relationship with scrubbing floors, she rolled up her sleeves and eased into a pair of rubber gloves to protect her hands. She loved the way the floors gleamed after a thorough cleaning, and the fresh lemony smell, barring the exhausting, manual labor that went with it.

Either way, she'd prayed over her decision to purchase the house, and with prayer came peace of mind. So she could do this. And she'd accept Keiran's help, because the financial savings would be tremendous.

That is, as long as he cut her a good deal, stayed in his attic apartment, and they maintained a working relationship.

And if he wasn't happy about that arrangement, he could book a hotel in town.

CHAPTER 2

After finishing a nitpicky adjustment to a kitchen remodeling project in Atlanta, Keiran O'Malley thanked the customer and gathered his tools as the other crewmen departed.

Done. Finally.

He drove his red pickup truck back to his apartment to finish packing, intentionally shifting his gaze away from the picturesque historic neighborhood of Iredell Park. Trendy and upscale, it had been reported as an up-and-coming neighborhood for young professionals. Many of the apartment buildings featured rooftop terraces, while several others were within walking distance of restaurants and shopping. He'd decided it would be an ideal area to live and raise a family.

And, he'd intended to set up a stand at the annual holiday display and sell his homemade Irish whiskey cake.

That was then, and this was now.

Still, they were everywhere—his shattered dreams. He shook his head, acknowledging that Atlanta held nothing for him anymore.

He slowed for the last turn to his apartment and went over what had happened that morning.

For once, he'd been able to complete a carpentry job on time and wasn't delayed because of Patricia, his ex-girlfriend. When they'd first met, he'd enjoyed her dark, sultry beauty.

Not any longer.

Usually, her compulsions to run in overdrive and make his life difficult were at the top of her priority list. Today she'd seemed preoccupied, although she'd slammed the office door in his face when he told her he was leaving Georgia for good.

Startled, he'd laughed and stared at the door. Really? As if this was all *his* fault?

He'd lifted his hand to knock. And then he'd pivoted and strode away. She was officially gone from his life. It was over. If only he could make peace with the fact that the two people he'd grown closest to—his girlfriend and his best friend, Kyle —had deceived him. They'd found each other and forgotten about him.

He bounded up the last flight of stairs and greeted Georges, his roommate, as he entered their fourth-floor walk-up apartment. They rented a place above a pawn shop, and Georges worked there part time, negotiating prices on the various items. Georges spent the rest of his time attending college online, majoring in international studies.

With a thump, Georges set a pizza box on the kitchen counter.

"I ordered pizza for my new roommate, Oscar." Georges's deep chuckle brought Keiran to the kitchen.

"Glad you found someone to take my place so quickly," Keiran said.

"Yup." Georges snatched a beer from the refrigerator and took a long swallow. "And we're planning to get blindingly drunk tonight."

"I hardly ever drink."

"Fortunately, Oscar drinks all the time. Take heart, *mon ami*. I'll miss your cooking." Georges headed to the living room and Keiran followed.

"That's my takeaway conversation?" Keiran asked.

"Most of it." Chuckling, Georges sank onto an armchair and drained his beer. "Because you're leaving, I'm putting take-out on speed-dial."

"Sorry, I don't deliver. You can always learn how to put together a casserole, or bake potatoes in a crockpot."

"Me? Every kitchen appliance runs when it sees me coming." Georges crooked a grin at the unlikely possibility of preparing a meal. "And I checked. Oscar doesn't even know how to fry an egg. He just drinks."

"Does he work?"

"He works at a law firm in town."

Impressed, Keiran inquired, "Is he a lawyer?"

"Nope. He works outside and struts around with a bill-board advertising their current specials—you know, divorces, insurance claims if you've been in an accident—"

"What kind of a lawyer does that?"

Georges barked a laugh. "The kind you call if you're in a jam. His firm is a one-stop shop kind of place. Oscar said the lawyer is also a locksmith. You've probably seen his advertising on TV. His name is Abraham Realgood and his nick-name is Honest Abe."

Unsuccessfully, Keiran tried to keep his face straight. "Well, thanks for an oversupply of information I'll never need."

"You never know when a lawyer is required, especially one who gets things done in a hurry." Georges lurched to his feet and the men shook hands, Georges joking all the while that he was charging his new roomie a higher rent for their "luxurious" studio apartment in the ancient building.

"You're a good guy, Keiran, and much more forgiving of Patricia and Kyle than I'd ever be," Georges said.

A good guy? Keiran thought.

Not particularly.

Forgiving?

Well, he embraced his faith. But if push came to shove, the answer would be *no*. He wasn't very forgiving.

"Always take the high road, son," his mother had often said.

I'm trying, Mom.

Wouldn't a good Christian man forgive an infidelity, as Georges believed Keiran had done?

Wishing his roommate well, Keiran packed his bags, hoisted his guitar case over his shoulder, and placed his father's precious football card in its plastic case. He tucked the deed to his family's pub, O'Malley's, into his wallet.

He loaded his belongings into his truck alongside the rest of the luggage he'd packed the evening before. Thirty minutes later, he headed east on I-85 through Georgia. He estimated it would take him less than four hours to reach Roses, North Carolina.

This was his opportunity to go back to his roots after leaving his family's pub far behind. He loved to cook and bake, and his father had discouraged him.

"I know the restaurant business," his father had lectured. "It's hard work, and I don't want you tied to a stove night and day, like me and your mother have been all these years. Pursue football. Go pro."

Keiran didn't have the desire, the instinct, or the talent to play football. He really liked the restaurant business. Each night, he'd link his hands behind his head and stare at the ceiling.

He couldn't follow his father's football dreams.

So instead, he'd reacted like an impetuous eighteen-year-old and left town. He'd follow his own road. He'd show his father he'd become a success without his family's support.

In Atlanta, he'd met Patricia. Soon afterward, she'd encouraged him to become a carpenter in her father's construction business, dreaming of million-dollar homes in stellar neighborhoods. Together, they'd climb the ladder of success. He'd learn the carpentry trade while she'd manage his appointments, advertise, and grow his business.

Young and trying to find his way, he'd responded with an enthusiastic "sure," and shelved the idea of opening a restaurant.

Now Patricia was gone and the ladder had been pulled out from under him.

In Roses, he'd be surrounded by the community that had given him an idyllic childhood. And maybe he could find his balance again—reopen the old family pub, visit Ireland for recipe inspirations. The more he thought about this new direction, the more he knew he had planned for the better.

He'd driven thirty minutes when Teddy Winchester phoned, introduced himself as a home flipper, and offered Keiran a job.

Keiran put his cellphone on speaker as Teddy explained that Desiree Contando, his sister-in-law, had purchased a Queen-Anne style home in Roses that was in a desperate state.

"Are you interested?" Teddy asked.

Keiran gripped the steering wheel. "How much repair?"

"I'm estimating a few months' worth. Do you have anything else lined up?"

"Not in the short term." Keiran reminded himself that there was more to life than dreams, and a steady income until he found his footing wasn't a bad idea.

"So will you take the job?"

"Without viewing it? What if your sister-in-law doesn't like my work?"

"She'll like it. Truth is, she's in a jam. The guy overseeing the project bailed, she's moving into 321 Thompson Lane today, and the place is a mess." Teddy paused. "Are you familiar with the road?"

"No, but I can find it."

"It's a definite fixer-upper. Despite that, the house has curb appeal and endless possibilities," Teddy continued in a distinct Southern drawl. "I learned from one of my crewmen that your craftmanship is excellent."

"Roses is my hometown and I'm headed back there as we speak," Keiran replied.

"Yes, so I've heard."

How had Teddy heard? Probably because men gossiped at twice the speed of women.

"As a bonus, I'll offer you an apartment—a remodel in the top dormer of her house. I lived there until my recent marriage and it's in good shape."

"What's the catch?" Keiran asked.

"I'm asking this favor because I sold Desiree the property," Teddy said. "Plus, I live two doors away."

"And you still want your wife speaking to you in the morning," Keiran finished with a laugh.

"Something like that."

"Sure, then," Keiran said. "I've been thinking a lot about making a difference in Roses."

Now why had he said that? Teddy was a stranger who offered employment, not his new buddy.

Serendipity. Fate. A coincidence. Keiran chose to believe the hand of God was bringing him back to his birthplace. A sign to leave his broken heart and Atlanta memories far behind.

Once the carpentry job was finished, he'd reopen his parents' pub. In the meantime, as a favor to Teddy for leading him to his first client, he'd give Desiree an excellent price.

"Thanks. I'll tell her to expect you," Teddy said. "Oh, and by the way, she works full time, so she won't be around much."

"What does she do?"

"She's a lawyer."

Smiling, Keiran clicked off his phone. A lawyer? Really? Two lawyer mentions in one day. He just hoped he never needed one.

He switched on the radio, bypassing the Christmas carols —the cheery "Santa Claus is Coming to Town" sung by a current rap star.

He settled on a classic contemporary station, and his fingers tapped a beat on the steering wheel as an 80's rock song belted, *"Don't stop believin'."* He knew the lyrics to the Journey hit by heart and sang along.

While sorting his collection of football cards, his father would hum the song after the pub closed for the evening. One particular card had been autographed by a well-known player, a guy he'd met while trying out for a first-pick college draft. His father hadn't made the cut. When Keiran had tried out for high school football, his father had given the prized card to him.

Keiran couldn't imagine his father as young and carefree, full of dreams and aspirations. He only remembered a man with a resigned look on his tired, worn face, his mother cooking diligently by his side.

Keiran glanced at his backpack holding the plastic-encased football card. "Thanks for giving me material things, Dad. I'm sorry I didn't live up to your ambitions. I only wish I had visited Ireland sooner to spend time with you."

But he hadn't.

"Don't stop believin'."

When the song ended, Keiran clicked off the radio, flicked on his left blinker, and exited the highway leading to Roses. He remembered the area, although he relied on his GPS to locate Thompson Lane.

He admired the natural scenery, the backdrop of the Blue Ridge Mountains, the celebratory way the town center was decked out for the holidays—the streetlights trimmed in decorative red bows, and the garlands strung along every shop's window box. He remembered his parents' love of Christmas had radiated throughout their pub, along with savory scents of homemade relishes, roasted turkeys, and exquisite caraway-seed-filled Irish desserts.

Once upon a time, he'd loved everything about Christmas. Now he was an adult, and the enchantment was gone. The constant arguments with Patricia had cured him of childhood expectations.

He parked at the curb in front of a ramshackle Queen-Anne style home at 321 Thompson Lane. The house stood like a freeze frame of a forgotten time.

"This must be the place," he murmured. He got out of his truck and surveyed the property. "A real fixer-upper, all right."

With his keen eye, Keiran assessed the exterior of the house against the fading afternoon light, grateful he'd arrived in Roses before dark. Patches of spongy moss grew along the slate roof. The window frames bubbled with fading beige paint. All these outdoor repairs would take hours of labor and he hadn't even stepped inside.

Despite the neglected appearance, the house brought back memories, and unexpected emotions rocked him. He recalled his childhood home in Roses, bordered by a white picket fence. The house had been located on the other side of town and was one of the largest in his neighborhood. In his mind, he heard his friends' laughter as they played kickball. He'd had no siblings, but had never felt lonely.

Beams of late afternoon sunshine streamed through the Queen Anne's front bay window. A recent rainfall brought a reflective gleam to the wavy glass. Raindrops trembled and shined along the yellow leaves on thick branches. The house was set in, canopied by four gigantic oak trees that appeared to be over a hundred years old.

Curb appeal, Teddy Winchester had said.

And a whole lot of work.

Keiran hesitated. He was a carpenter, not a demolition crew.

Unlimited possibilities.

Well, that one was negotiable, and depended on how much repair the house required. It certainly exuded charm and a salute to a bygone era. He just had to have faith that the bygone era wasn't so long ago that the home offered no modern comforts.

He didn't blink, hardly moving, debating. A slight drizzle from the tree leaves coated his cheeks and two days' worth of dark stubble. There were no lights on inside the home, although the flicker of candlelight illuminated a window.

He scrubbed a hand over his face, then retrieved his backpack, guitar, and toolbox from his truck. He'd get the rest of his luggage later.

Again, he stared at the house.

He was here, had driven all afternoon, and it seemed foolish not to see if Desiree was home. He went to the front door and knocked once.

No answer.

Twice.

No answer.

He debated about clicking the brass handle to check if the

door was locked. But, even if it was, he couldn't exactly stroll inside.

On the third knock, the door abruptly opened, and he came face to face with a beautiful woman with deep-set blue eyes. She held a lighted candle, sheltering the flickering glow with her small, cupped hand. She could have stepped out of a fairy tale—Cinderella came to mind. Her thick blond hair was piled on top of her head, held precariously by a blue headband. Her fair complexion was smudged with dirt.

"Desiree Contando?" he asked. He thought she flinched, but assumed he was mistaken.

"Just Desiree, please." The expression on her oval-shaped face was calm, and her hair shone in the last rays of daylight. Slender, she wore a pair of worn denims and a plaid flannel shirt with the sleeves rolled up.

A spin of warmth between them sparked an attraction he hadn't expected.

She was drop-dead gorgeous, especially if a guy was drawn to fairytale princesses.

He apparently was. Although he'd tried dating a princess and had failed spectacularly. Patricia had never been happy, despite his attempts to shower her with compliments, expensive meals, and flowers whenever he could afford them.

In the end, it was obvious their values and interests didn't match, and she'd discarded him for his wealthy best friend. Aye, she wanted the castle and the crown. She didn't have time to waste on a guy trying to figure out if he wanted to be a carpenter or a cook.

"Hi, Desiree." Spellbound, he just stared. She had the prettiest golden hair, framing a perfect complexion and generous mouth.

She blinked and took a step back. "Mr. O'Malley?"

"Keiran."

"I've been expecting you." Her tone was dispassionate as

she gestured with her small chin to the home's worn interior. "My brother-in-law said you were driving from Atlanta."

A breeze shifted, the wind carrying the promise of chilly winter nights to come. "Yes, all afternoon."

The weariness in her blue eyes deepened. "Do you realize what you're getting into here?"

"Absolutely." He nodded reassuringly. "I'm a carpenter, more or less."

"With any luck, it's more rather than less. This house warrants an excellent carpenter, plus a whole lot more." Her expression tightened. "Are you also a licensed electrician? I've lost power."

"No," he admitted.

The candle wavered in her hand, vulnerable to the late afternoon breeze.

She shrugged. "Then your services aren't required tonight."

"I was told I had a place to stay when I got here," he said.

"Yes, once you begin working. However, there's nothing for you to do yet, and because it's my first night in my new home, I'd prefer to spend it alone. I'll see you in the morning—and bring an electrician with you." She stepped back and closed the door.

"Well, that's perfect." He stared at the wooden front door, then down at the sagging porch. Evidently, this was his day for women opting to slam the door in his face. "I came all this way, but because I'm not the acceptable tradesman for this evening, I'm supposed to sleep in my truck," he muttered. His earlier enthusiasm at arriving in Roses was quickly waning.

You were planning to come, anyway, a small voice in his head reminded him. *You were going to take a ride by your parents' deserted pub, then find a place to stay in town.*

Aye, before Teddy's phone call.

Nevertheless . . .

He was still muttering when the door opened.

"Mr. O'Malley, are you talking to my porch?" Desiree asked.

"Just enjoying my visit with your broken-down floor. That is, when I'm not having a conversation with the rusty propane grill in the corner." He kept his focus downward. "This porch is unsteady. You'd better hope it doesn't cave in, or you'll be clamoring for a carpenter faster than you can say Queen-Anne disaster."

"Are you saying my house might collapse?" She laughed, and that amazed him. It was unexpected. She seemed so serious, with her slim shoulders and strong posture, her huge eyes speaking of sadness. Slight shadows beneath her eyes gave her an unconscious vulnerability, and one, he guessed, she would never admit to.

Her laugh seemed stilted, though. Just like his had been that morning with Patricia. An ironic laugh of disbelief.

"Minor setbacks. Everything can be fixed." He plastered on a reassuring grin that he didn't quite feel. "We'll bring your house back to her former majestic state."

"For now, she's a good distance from her former crown." Desiree smiled, and this time her smile seemed more genuine. "Why are you still standing on my porch, Mr. O'Malley?"

He studied the lit candle in her hand, and then her. She looked absolutely exquisite, her high cheekbones accentuated by pink color, her classic beauty understated. She wore no makeup, and reminded him of a master painting by Raphael—*Woman with a Veil* came to mind. Alluringly beautiful.

Before answering, he questioned himself. Why *was* he still here? Did he truly belong in Roses? Was he good enough to transform a house in shambles into splendor? Was he good enough to open his parents' pub, a legacy he didn't deserve?

A part of him said aye, although it had nothing to do with the house. Or the pub, for that matter. He wanted to learn more about Desiree Contando.

Not a good idea. Wrong reasons. He was here to work. Besides, he was spinning off of a bad relationship. Better to wall himself off from all women, especially attractive women with enchanting eyes and enticing lips.

He was amazed by his next response, which had nothing to do with his thoughts. "This is my hometown and I haven't been back in ten years. Give me a chance."

"I will, in the morning."

"I would've booked a room in town if I'd known." He pulled out his cell phone. "I'll call Morrison's Hotel on Main Street."

"They closed five years ago."

He didn't think twice. There was Broad Acres, a bed and breakfast on the outskirts. He told her as much.

"They shut down last year," came her cool reply.

He clapped a hand to his forehead. "So here I stand, wondering where I'll be sleeping tonight. Teddy mentioned he lived a couple of doors down. Last name is Winchester?"

"Yes, and ... no. I mean, don't call him." Desiree's tone stayed no-nonsense. "He and my sister, Candee, are newlyweds. Plus, they're raising a young boy."

"I'll snooze in my truck for the night, then." Keiran picked up his things. "I've slept in worse places."

"Have you?" Desiree assessed him. "From what I recall, only the finest was good enough for a guy like you."

He grimaced at her evaluation. "Do we know each other, Desiree?"

"I know *of* you. I first saw you at a high school football game. Your nickname was Richie Rich."

Wow, was he ever tired of people assessing him on the basis of his well-to-do background. Sure, his parents had been wealthy and he'd never lacked for anything, although they'd toiled long hours for their success. With the same work ethic, he'd driven himself hard in order to prove himself among the other tradesmen in Atlanta.

He held her gaze. "Rich doesn't mean lazy."

"Not always." Those two words, a slight concession, an assessment of a guy she'd labeled without any facts. Frustration mushroomed inside him.

"Did we talk?" he asked.

"Where?"

"At the football game."

"Are you kidding?" She avoided his gaze. "You were too busy with the pretty cheerleader."

"I can't remember her name."

Desiree started to scowl, but chuckled when he did.

"Do you remember mine?" she asked.

He held out his hand. "I don't think we were ever formally introduced. Let's try this again. I'm Keiran, Desiree."

She accepted his handshake. Her hand was fine and delicate. The idea of living in her house was becoming incredibly appealing.

"So you're an authority about me based on a high school football game?" He still held her hand. She made no move to let go. Neither did he.

Silence reigned for a beat.

Quietly, she shifted her stance and pulled her hand from his. "True. Sometimes one chapter doesn't mean you read the whole book."

"Precisely."

Sure, he'd made bad choices. He'd been foolish and reckless for leaving a town he loved in order to prove he could make it on his own, falling into a profession totally removed from the restaurant scene.

She trained her attention on him, her deep-set eyes considering. "Teddy predicts this house will take several months to complete. I'm hoping he's wrong."

Keiran hoped Teddy was right.

"Hard to tell until I see it." He stamped his feet on the dog-eared welcome mat, a not-so-subtle hint. "May I come in? It's cold out here."

"Why not?" She brushed those gorgeous waves from her face. "After you, Mr. O'Malley." With a graceful turn, she ushered him inside.

CHAPTER 3

Desiree led the way through the foyer, pausing to peer at a silvery spider web, an excuse to gain two seconds to compose herself. She'd been totally unprepared. She needed time for this new development she hadn't expected.

And that development was Keiran O'Malley. The handsome, dashing Irish football player. She was certain he was accustomed to plush surroundings, and her house was the farthest one could get from that scenario.

Seeing him, she'd done a double-take, surprised that he surpassed her adolescent daydreams. In high school, she'd heard that he lived on the south side of town, the wealthy side, where tall privacy hedges bordered the homes.

A decade had passed and he'd grown even more striking. His teen body had filled out, and tiny crinkles had formed around his Prince Charming green eyes. The navy-blue parka he wore accentuated his athletic shoulders.

His family had reached financial success owning their profitable pub until it abruptly closed. After Keiran departed (she'd inquired), the pub had gone into a downward slide and never recovered from the economic recession.

The way her heart had thudded when she saw him reminded her that her youthful crush was alive and well. Definitely, she should keep her distance. Difficult to accomplish when she couldn't keep her eyes off him.

She realized his gaze was assessing her, from her messy hair to her disheveled jeans and oversized flannel shirt.

Ten years. During that time she'd earned a bachelor's degree, followed by three years of law school and passed the arduous bar exam on her first try.

Every day since then, she'd had a single-minded vision of creating a picture-perfect life. Her own childhood had been just the opposite. However, she'd learned that as an adult, she could control her destiny. Especially with perseverance and God's generosity.

At present, she focused on the monumental task ahead—transforming a rapidly deteriorating house into the holiday fantasy of her dreams.

"This is lovely," Keiran said.

She swallowed as her gaze shifted to his finely chiseled features. "You're being serious?"

"Aye. The house has good bones. And we'll be able to build on that."

"Speedily, I hope," came her patented reply.

He lifted a dark eyebrow. "In six months this place will be as good as new."

"Six months? I'm hosting Christmas Eve dinner and the kitchen needs to be ready by then."

He gave her a skeptical look. "Does your oven function?" he asked.

"Function? Hah! Fortunately, Christmas Eve isn't tomorrow. I've . . . *we've* got a few weeks."

"To perform a miracle?" He motioned to the mismatched wallpaper in the foyer, the floorboards desperate for major repair, and narrowed his gaze. For a split second, she thought he might turn around and leave.

Purposefully, she didn't meet his stare. "Only God performs miracles."

"Glad we agree on something," he replied. "Six months is a generous estimate and the renovation may take much longer depending on any unforeseen problems once we get started." He set his backpack, guitar, and toolbox in the foyer. "Many times, remodeling goes weeks slower than a customer anticipates. Unexpected delays and spiraling costs are part of the process. When was this house built?"

She rolled her eyes. "Many years ago."

"Please let me know when you find out." He crossed his arms. Tall, athletic, and vital, with his male-model good looks and utterly appealing smile, he was definitely out of place in her shabby interior. He should have been strolling across a Dublin runway wearing designer clothes, not standing in her rundown foyer in worn jeans and a navy-blue parka.

"Surely the age of a home doesn't determine the renovation," she snapped at him, and felt churlish for snapping. Having him stand a few inches away sent unexpected tingles through her nerves. Long ago, she'd secured a place in her heart for him and only him. To have the object of her affection so near made her want to confess her infatuation. Blurt it out and get it over with, so he wouldn't think she was bad mannered for gaping and hesitating and staring.

Whoa. Hold that thought. They'd been together ten minutes and she wanted to tell him how much she'd dreamed about him ten years ago.

No, no, no. She was obviously overtired.

He didn't reply. Instead, he headed for the kitchen. "Other

tradesmen will factor in their estimates and might not cut you the same once-in-a-lifetime deal I'm giving you, and there may be surprises in older homes." He swiped a finger across the double-paneled wainscoting in the adjoining pantry.

That was one of the reasons she loved this house, because of the exquisite detailing not found in cookie-cutter newer homes.

"What kind of surprises?" she asked.

"Termite damage and rotting plumbing, to name a couple."

She winced. Unexpected problems would put a definite crimp in her bank account. "What is your once-in-a-lifetime deal, by the way?"

He paused to check a loose floorboard. "You'll need to trust me."

Easy to say, but words were cheap. She frowned and eyed his strong shoulders.

"Should I start on the renovations tonight?" He pulled off his parka, exposing thick arm muscles bulging from a cream-colored T-shirt. "I feel like I should at least fix that loose wire in your foyer because you're letting me bunk here a day early."

"Sure. Great. Thanks." She had to stop gazing at him.

He'd be sleeping in the attic, which was one floor above her bedroom. She'd hear his footsteps padding across the floor, the water running in the small shower when he bathed. Her heart beat quicker in her chest. This was her teenage dream come true, except the dream was several years too late.

Determined to ignore his desirability, she swallowed hard. Her gaze transferred to the kitchen counter. "Have you eaten?"

"Nope." He peered past her. "Any chance the stove or microwave works?"

"Both appliances are in terrible shape and should be ripped out. Plus, there's no power tonight so you're out of luck." She drew a breath. "Do you cook?"

"My parents owned a pub."

She knew that and waited for him to elaborate. When he didn't, she offered, "My sister brought muffins."

"What kind?"

"Pumpkin. Now you're being selective?" She pointed to the refrigerator. "And there's bottled water in the fridge."

"Any idea when the power will be back on?"

"I checked my phone for an update. A storm hit farther north and affected the lines in this area. The power company estimated everything should be fixed by nightfall."

"Excellent."

Excellent. Excellent would be reporting to her law firm tomorrow morning and coming back home in the evening to a fixed, finished house all decorated for Christmas. Excellent would be keeping her personal life private by living in her own space, far from the gaze of her swoon-worthy new roommate.

She ran a hand through her disheveled curls, wishing she'd pulled a comb through her hair before he'd arrived. And why hadn't she changed back into the proper business suit she'd worn earlier?

Keiran washed his hands in the sink. He slanted a glance at her while grabbing a bottle of water. "You want anything?"

She shook her head, her gaze dropping to her waistline. "After the Thanksgiving holiday, I intend to eat light for the next few weeks."

His gaze did likewise, and he smiled broadly. "You look great to me."

Her heart took a leap.

All day, her emotions had roller-coasted from exhilaration to anxiety. Now, as she stared up at the rugged dark-haired man who seemed sincere in his compliment, unexpected tears sprang to her eyes.

"This has been a difficult week," she admitted. "Usually I can juggle a lot of things with ease—"

"Difficult because of Thanksgiving and working full time? Teddy said you're a lawyer."

His question was so unexpected, so gentle, she smiled despite the tears. "No. Thanksgiving was wonderful. My sister Candee, or rather Teddy, cooked a Thanksgiving feast —a turkey with all the trimmings." She didn't tell him that she and Candee had never experienced a normal Thanksgiving growing up, so they savored every festive get-together. They knew what it was like to go without.

"Holidays are good." Lightly, he covered her hand with his fingers. "They're meant to be enjoyed with loved ones."

Awareness of his masculine presence stirred her pulse. "Mr. O'Malley—"

"Keiran."

She opened her mouth to object, then thought better of it. "Keiran, then."

"Now we're equals, Desiree." Although his tone teased, his expression turned serious.

They were hardly equals. He'd been born with the proverbial silver spoon in his mouth. She'd been born into squalor.

"I . . . I assume your Thanksgiving in Atlanta was pleasant," she offered.

He hesitated, then let out a brief sigh. "I cooked a turkey, a sweet potato casserole, and a round Irish cake filled with caraway seeds for me and my roommate."

"Wow. You'll be a welcome addition to any gathering."

So he'd had a roommate. A woman? she wondered, although she didn't ask.

"I never learned how to fix a proper meal, and now my life is hectic." Despite her shrug, she couldn't quite hold the apology from her voice, although she questioned what she was apologizing for. She hadn't had the opportunity to cook in her foster homes. More often than not, she'd been relegated to a spare room and ignored.

"My favorite pastime is spending afternoons in the kitchen trying new recipes," he said.

"I thought you were a carpenter. I imagined you crafting items out of wood."

He met her gaze. "A guy can do more than one thing, Desiree."

"But can he do more than one thing well?"

"Can you?"

"Absolutely."

"Then so can I." Approval and mirth brightened his face. His hand still covered hers. "Also, I make a mean Irish whiskey cake."

"I bake a pistachio cake that is usually edible, as long as I don't forget it's in the oven."

"How can you forget a cake? Don't you set a kitchen timer?"

"Sometimes." Another shrug. "Believe me, a cake in the oven is easy to forget, especially when I'm immersed in a court case and bring the work home with me. When that happens, I get sidetracked."

He laughed. "When your oven is fixed, we'll set a timer so your cake won't burn, and then I'll challenge you to a baking contest."

"Oh really. Who will be the judge?"

His gaze lit with sharpened interest. "Does Roses still hold a holiday cake contest on the village green?"

"Yes." She acknowledged his question with a smirk. "And always the weekend before Christmas."

"I thought so."

"I'm certain your cake will be a success."

"And so will yours."

She chuckled. "I highly doubt it."

He nodded.

Why was she able to fall into such easy conversation with him when they'd only talked for a short time? He seemed genuinely interested.

Not romantically, though.

No. Guys from his wealthy background didn't give the time of day to women like her.

Still, what was she doing? The peaceful intimacy of his large hand on hers caused her to relax a little too much. However attractive, this man was her employee, and their arrangement was strictly business.

She jerked her hand away.

He didn't seem to notice.

With a flash of white teeth, he offered that devastating grin again. "Do you accept my challenge?" he asked.

"To bake?"

"Aye. I'll make it official. I challenge you to the Roses Christmas baking contest."

"That's not fair. Your parents owned a pub."

"A pub isn't the corner bakery."

"You have more experience in a kitchen than me."

He winked. "I'll teach you all I know."

Cozy evenings baking homemade Christmas treats with him? Immediately, her heart agreed. Her common sense, however, reminded her this wasn't a good idea.

At any rate, she couldn't keep from chuckling and

accepting the challenge. His enthusiasm was contagious, and besides, what was the problem with gaining another ten pounds? Hah! She'd simply buy the next size up in clothes or scope out an elastic waistband.

"We'll schedule oven rights while you're here," she said.

"Sounds good."

Warmth bloomed in her cheeks as she gazed at him. Keiran O'Malley was a strong-featured, devastatingly attractive man who liked to cook and bake. Heads would certainly turn when he strode through town, especially if he toted a cartful of his homemade Irish whiskey cakes.

Opening the bakery box on the counter, he offered her a muffin. She declined and he chose one for himself. The table held a smattering of stoneware, along with boxes of utensils. She intended to arrange the glass-paned cupboards with an artful display of dishes and decided to get started while he ate.

Carefully, she corralled a stack of plates and mounted a chair. At her petite height, she stood on her toes to reach the top shelf of the cupboard.

"Get rid of the doors," he said.

She twisted toward him. "I'm sorry?"

"And lime green isn't trending these days."

"Just like that?" His confident attitude annoyed her. "Doesn't my opinion count? I *am* the owner."

"Of course." He waved a hand around. "Though in the latest designs, kitchens are painted white. And for a more open quality, remove the cupboard doors."

Plates in hand, she remained standing on the chair. "I've already decided to paint the walls dove white. I may want to leave the cupboard doors intact, though, so don't go throwing anything into the junk pile without my permission."

He nodded. "At least wait a few days before you decide."

Digesting his information, she agreed as he helped her off the chair. She loved an open floor plan, and took notes while she watched the home improvement TV shows for modern-day ideas.

While he leaned against the sink, she relit several candles. His gaze assessed her, assessed her kitchen, assessed the flickering candlelight.

She ran warm, sudsy water into the sink and placed several dusty dishes to soak. "You still haven't told me how much the renovation will cost."

Slowly, he bit into the muffin, chewed, swallowed, and took a swig of water. "I haven't seen your house yet."

"You're standing in the main room. Surely you have a rough estimate in your head."

A winning smile lit his features. "A million dollars, give or take a hundred thousand."

"That's not funny."

"I'll know better after you show me around." He strode into the foyer for his toolbox. "First, I'll fix that loose wire hanging from your ceiling."

"You're not an electrician."

"I learned a few things while working on construction sites all these years." He pulled a screwdriver from his toolbox.

"Do you know what you're doing?" She hurried after him. "I don't want you electrocuted before you begin working tomorrow."

He stopped dead and directed a grin at her. "If that happens, your repair list might be delayed a few days."

"You're brimming with not-so-funny jokes today."

"How's this?" he asked. "Providing I'm okay, I'll whip you up an omelet. I noticed you have a dozen eggs in your refrigerator."

"The stove isn't working."

"There's a grill on your front porch. If you have a cast-iron frying pan in one of those boxes, we're all set."

She burst out laughing as mixed reactions filled her. Keiran O'Malley embodied the best qualities in a man. And no matter how much she'd questioned his expertise, he was rapidly becoming a true blessing.

CHAPTER 4

A week passed, bringing the first Friday in December to a close. Along with record-breaking cold temperatures, the promise of snow was in the air, and daylight hours were rapidly becoming shorter.

Despite her desire to snuggle indoors and eat platefuls of carbohydrates, Desiree's over-filled schedule demanded she spend her days at her law firm filing last-minute appeals. Hours, days, had gone by in a blur, and she hadn't devoted as much time as she'd initially earmarked for remodeling her new home. As a lawyer fighting for those who couldn't afford it, she knew her service was critical. Many parents were without the financial means to support themselves or their children, and some spouses were victims of domestic violence. On numerous occasions, she'd provided free legal assistance by working pro bono.

At half past seven in the evening, she eased her car into her gravel driveway. During the day, a number of pickup trucks parked there, although all the tradesmen clocked out by three-thirty. Not Keiran, of course. Keiran worked nonstop.

A light drizzle wet the streets, and she yearned for snow—to sit lightly on her eyelashes, to gift wrap the magical season of Christmas.

She stepped onto the front porch, which Keiran had fixed, and admired the pine-scented, evergreen wreath strung with holly berries and pinecones.

"The first sign of Christmas." He greeted her with a lopsided grin as she opened the front door and smacked into him. Through the thin denim of his shirt, his body was warm, his broad chest hard and toned. She gazed up at his thick midnight-black hair, his well-defined features, and took in a sharp breath.

The smile on his face changed from humor to something else. Something deeper. He gazed at her lips, and she instinctively held her breath. His daily presence in her life was a sweet enticement she refused to acknowledge, and it took all her effort to resist his magnetism.

He dusted off his hands, then took her wool coat and set it on a hallway chair.

The renovation had come an incredibly long way in the short time since he'd arrived, and she peered around approvingly. Although she'd immediately wanted to shop for paint swatches, he'd advised focusing on the practical rather than the aesthetic. The roof, windows, and masonry repairs came first. The house required secure sealing, especially with winter approaching.

She'd approved, and in the course of a few days he'd taken on the role as general contractor, quickly becoming fast friends with Teddy. Keiran relied on Teddy's expertise, as well as his contacts. Once the house was watertight, he'd enlisted a crew to sand and sheetrock the kitchen walls.

As she did every evening upon entering the foyer, she peered at the ceiling and muttered, "Eventually, I'm getting rid of that hideous gold fixture."

"I like it." Keiran came to stand beside her. The harsh light of the open bulbs splayed across his face, and she reached up to brush a trace of sawdust from his cheeks.

He caught her hand, squeezing it warmly. "How was your day?"

"Busy. Yours?"

"The same. And I wouldn't have it any other way."

They'd come to an amiable understanding. He'd maintained a professional, friendly distance and, consequently, they'd built a trusting friendship. Somehow, he'd known intuitively that that was the relationship she wanted, and he'd quickly adapted to her unspoken request.

Her gaze swept the foyer, coming to rest on the hardwood floor. "Can the unevenness be fixed?" she asked.

"Any problem can be fixed. The question is, can you live with an imbalanced floor? I checked with a professional and the house's structure is okay, so I'd leave it and save the money." He gestured toward the bay window in the living room. "Same with the wavy glass. These qualities add character to an older home."

"Beautiful imperfections," she mused. "Like people."

"Perfectly imperfect, my chaplain in Atlanta preached at Sunday services," Keiran replied. "People are setting their sights on happiness, but searching in the wrong places. None of us, and nothing we create, is perfect. We expect a lot of others, though."

"And of ourselves," she said. "It may be that perfection isn't always the best way."

"Better to get over ourselves and think more about serving the people in our lives."

She nodded, reflecting, knowing she was forever striving to create a textbook world for herself, the one she'd read about in fables when she was a child.

Nonetheless, attaining the accomplishments her friends

often displayed on social media brought about exhaustion. Consequently, she didn't enjoy the here and now.

"Wise words," she replied.

And Keiran personified those words. He acted knowledgeably and humbly, and performed his work with a consideration that made her admire the person he was—kind, steadfast, and capable.

Each evening, he'd help her unpack endless boxes and order takeout, with a promise to cook her a proper meal once the stove and oven were installed. In the meantime, he'd rearranged her meager furniture and added a touch she would have expected more from a professional decorator than a carpenter with no formal design training.

"My chaplain is an inspiring person," he went on. "If you're ever free on a weekend, I can bring you to a church service in Atlanta. The drive takes a few hours, although it's doable in one day."

She gazed at him, and pretended she didn't. Her first inclination was to immediately decline his invitation, to maintain their cool, professional relationship.

But how could she?

She could hardly feign disinterest in this six-foot-two man with sparkling green eyes and an utterly masculine appeal. She loved talking with him, laughing with him. And she was impressed by his attention to elements and setup. He had an excellent discernment for arrangement, and was resourceful and creative, keeping her strict budget in mind at all times.

A fun conversationalist, he sported a keen knowledge in topics ranging from child advocacy to football, and, of course, cooking and baking. All in all, she considered him a Renaissance man, a term she'd once heard applied to a man blessed with intellect and proficient in a wide range of areas.

Although the term had originated in Italy, with his mesmerizing charm, Keiran was the epitome of the quick-witted Irish male.

"How's the kitchen coming?" she asked as she set down her briefcase.

"I was waiting for you to ask. Quicker than I anticipated, thanks to Teddy's efficient crew. The walls are painted, and your new appliances were delivered and installed this morning." As always, every sentence he uttered was enhanced by a hand gesture. "Do you want to see it?"

"Of course."

"Close your eyes." Obediently, she squeezed her eyes shut as he led her down the hallway.

He gave her hand a light squeeze. "Open."

She stopped at the kitchen entryway and gasped. Surely, this wasn't the same kitchen that had resembled a demolition area only a few days before.

As she and Keiran had discussed, the walls had been painted a dove white, and shiny new countertops were set in marbled granite. The white freestanding farmhouse sink was a surprise, paired with an old-world style pull-down faucet. A glossy tiled backsplash completed the ambience, along with open cupboards. She'd taken his advice and discarded the doors, giving the space a fluid, chic design.

He gestured to an empty corner. "A base cabinet is on backorder. Once it arrives, I'll install it. Hopefully it will be here in time for Christmas."

She sighed dreamily. "Thank you."

Her kitchen was exactly how she'd envisioned it, and a trendsetter's dream. Natural light spilled inside, thanks to sliding glass doors leading to her two-acre plot of land. A consistent thread of sunny yellow complemented the shelving rims, which were the colors they'd agreed upon. An oversized island in a high-gloss finish created a work triangle between the stove and refrigerator and seamlessly accommodated gleaming stainless-steel appliances. Her kitchen table and chairs had been tucked beneath a set of framed picture windows.

Awestruck, she put her fingers to her mouth. "All you've done in a week is more than most contractors could accomplish in a month."

He laughed. "The credit goes to Teddy's large, efficient crew. I'm merely one person supervising the project and helping wherever warranted."

"Truly, you are a genius."

He gazed down at her with tender amusement. "And while I was overseeing the renovations, you were protecting innocent children. If anyone deserves praise, Desiree, it's you."

Her heart skipped a beat.

Retrieving her coat, he strode to the hallway closet while she kicked off her black leather pumps, pulled on her favorite cardigan, and claimed a stool at the counter. She breathed in the aroma of seafood chowder simmering on the stove, and the sweet, enticing scent of a cake rising in the oven.

"And, in addition to the remodeling, you cooked?" she asked.

"Seafood chowder was my parents' signature dish. During my lunch hour, I shopped for the ingredients. For dessert, I baked an Irish whiskey cake."

"The very same cake you're challenging me with for the baking contest on the village green? It's totally not fair if you get a head start."

"I'll make it up to you."

She crossed her arms. "How?"

"We'll shop for a Christmas tree tomorrow, and I'm

buying. Only a ten-foot spruce will complement your living room's high ceilings. Aye?"

"Aye." How could she refuse a hardworking Irishman? In fascinated admiration, she watched him snap up a wooden spoon and adeptly stir the chowder.

"We'll eat dinner together after I shower and change?" he asked.

"Sure. Everything is wonderful."

He chuckled. "Brilliant."

A jumble of sensations made her pause. No man had ever cooked dinner for her before, inquired about her day, or taken a sincere interest. His consideration went way beyond their work relationship.

She stood and took a bottled water from the refrigerator. "Don't you have anywhere else you'd rather be on a Friday night?"

He studied her face, came closer, then pressed a light kiss on her forehead. "The more time I spend with you, the more time I want to spend with you. Does that make sense?"

There was no reason to offer a blasé answer, so she nodded a yes, because it made perfect sense. That pure attraction for him, a feeling she couldn't shake. Enjoy the moment, she told herself.

The thought made her absurdly pleased.

As he made for the stairs, she paused to take in the splendor of her polished, cheery kitchen. Previously, Keiran had drawn a sketch on his computer and gotten her approval, and his ideas had panned out. Ensuring the interior wall wasn't load-bearing, Teddy's crew had torn down the wall between the kitchen and dining room to make the most of her square footage.

A large communal area for family and friends was ideal for entertaining, Keiran had said.

She hadn't purchased a dining room set, and didn't foresee one in her immediate future.

Smiling, she arranged place settings on the kitchen island using her good china dishes and silver flatware. She'd started a hope chest when she graduated from college. It was silly, and most people had never heard of one. Despite her difficult upbringing, she believed in love and marriage, and a future with a special man. Starry-eyed dreams, she contemplated, while she folded white cloth napkins.

Keiran was down the stairs fifteen minutes later in his favorite pair of lived-in jeans and a T-shirt that revealed his fit physique. His thick jet-black hair was still wet from a shower, and he hadn't bothered to shave. His stubbled chin and prominent cheekbones made her pause. And his scent . . .

Oh, my. Now he even smelled like an Irishman—like early morning and whistle clean.

He raised a questioning dark eyebrow over his teasing gaze. "You own a service of fine crystal and china, your dining area is large enough for a twenty-person feast, and there's no place to sit and enjoy a meal?"

"Pull up a stool, like I did." She nodded to the island. "Or I'll pile cushions on the floor and we'll sit cross-legged. Someday, when I win the lottery, I'll buy dining room furniture."

He regarded the brass flush-mount light above the island. "What type of fixture do you want there?"

"I love French country design." She bent to a stack of magazines she kept in a wicker basket in the corner, and thumbed through one. "I saw a distressed frame fixture with candelabra detailing. See?"

He peered over her shoulder. "Excellent taste. I approve of all you've done." His breath was warm and tickled her ear.

That pull again, drawing her to him.

"You mean, all *you've* done," she corrected.

His lips twitched. Reaching up to the cupboard, he brought out two wine glasses. "I also bought a bottle of sparkling cider for our date."

"You're categorizing eating seafood chowder together at home as kind of a date?"

"Not kind of a date. It is a date."

"Is it a proper date?"

He sobered. "No. But it's here and now and let's embrace the moment."

Her heart did a double-turn in her chest. She didn't want this. Someday . . . maybe . . . when her house was finished and her career was established. And that would take years. Slowly, she was working her way up the ranks, though she owed thousands of dollars in student loans.

Besides, Keiran lived here. Did that count as a date?

At any rate, the man in question strode to the stove and stirred buttery seafood chowder with a wooden spoon.

"Want a taste?" he asked. "I baked a loaf of soda bread to mop up the soup. It's sitting on the table in a wicker bread basket I found in your cupboard."

"Okay, now you're showing off," she teased.

A chuckle tugged at the corners of his mouth. "Do you like the appliances?" As he stirred, he gestured to the six-burner stove and double oven. "Exactly what you ordered."

She kept herself from staring at him by concentrating on slicing the bread.

"It's impressive," she said. "And the low price Teddy's warehouse supplier gave for the cabinets was a relief. A huge thank you."

She'd taken out a home equity loan in addition to her mortgage to cover the improvements. Although she was realistic enough to understand she wasn't financially equipped to afford a total house renovation, she presumed the kitchen and bathrooms were most important. To save money, they'd concentrated on what Keiran labeled "mid-range renovations." He'd upgraded the countertops and changed the lighting.

"You're welcome," he said. "My pleasure, Desiree."

"A modern kitchen has always been my fantasy."

His gaze locked with hers. "Do you have other . . . fantasies?"

You, she almost said aloud. Swallowing, she pushed her gaze to his Irish whiskey cake baking in the oven. She whistled lightly and adeptly changed the subject. "Tell me again how you managed to get all this done, plus bake a cake."

"I delegate." He lifted a clean spoon from a drawer and scooped several spoonfuls of the chowder into a bowl, then brought the bowl to her for a taste. "I learned the skill from my father. When you own a pub, you can't do everything yourself."

She savored the hearty taste of cream, corn and potatoes blended with tender clams and sweet red peppers. "Mmm," she murmured. "This is delicious."

"A secret family recipe."

"Really? You won't share your recipe?"

"It's been handed down through several generations." He watched her, and his gaze shifted to her mouth. Gently, without warning, he kissed her. "Although I can assure you that the chowder isn't nearly as delicious as you."

The oven timer dinged. Reluctantly, he about-faced and gripped a mitt by the stove. He pulled out the cake and set it on a trivet.

"I'll glaze it in a few days. I'm testing a new glaze recipe." He gestured to the sugar and butter glaze, blended with whiskey, and grabbed a spoon so she could taste it.

"More deliciousness," she said softly.

He didn't mention the kiss. It had been quick and light. And memorable.

They'd fallen into a pattern of spending their evenings together, and her first home-cooked meal in her new home proved a mouthwatering delight. After slicing his cake, still warm from the oven, for a "taste test," they washed and dried Desiree's fine china and crystal by hand.

Afterward, Keiran led her into the living room, where he pointed out the detailing on the marble fireplace. Pausing, he got to his knees and inspected the chimney.

"I thought we'd light a fire again tonight," he said. "Eventually, you'll need a chimney sweep. Until then, the fireplace is safe to use."

"Teddy lit the fireplace several times when he lived here," she said.

Still on his knees, Keiran glanced up at her. "So is that a yes? Aye?" When she nodded, he gestured to the matches on the mantel and she handed them to him.

"The crew and I checked your central heating system too," he said, as he lit a match and checked the draft.

"Don't tell me, let me guess. The entire unit died."

"Aye, but don't worry." He offered a reassuring nod. "Fortunately, a reasonably priced HVAC guy stopped over. He's one of Teddy's crewmen."

"How much does a new HVAC cost?"

"Depends on the square footage of the house." Keiran lit the fire and waited for the logs to burn before standing. "I'd estimate your house is around three thousand square feet."

"You're right on target."

"Then your unit will cost six thousand dollars." He gave her the box of matches, his rough fingers brushing against hers. An electric current passed between them, and she felt that insistent magnetism. Not the youthful yearnings of an adolescent. On the contrary, hers were the dreams of a grown woman.

Instinctively, she pulled her hand away and wandered to the bay window. Outside, the vibrant colors of a Carolina winter day had faded, and twilight merged to darkness. The pavement gleamed with the slickness of a wet evening.

Across the street, Mr. Juno, a graduate student with a young family, had decorated his porch with an impressively lit display. Gold, red, and green boxes, wrapped in dazzling silver ribbons and bows, glowed with Christmas color and light.

She wiped unexpected tears from the corners of her eyes. What was it about Christmas that always got to her? Was it because she'd never experienced a real celebration because of her alcoholic parents? Because she'd never had a truly loving home? When life was bleakest, she'd searched for the warmth of faith and community. The Yuletide season was a time of celebration, just never for her and her sister. At least, not until this past year when Candee had married Teddy, and Desiree had purchased her first home.

"Desiree, I realize you're overwhelmed because of the renovations, but everything will evolve into the home of your dreams. I promise." Keiran came to stand behind her. His voice was sincere and deep, and a heat of longing pulsed in her veins. She blamed it on the romance of the candlelight, the flames flickering in the fireplace, the patter of raindrops on the bay window.

With its poignant reminders of the approaching holiday, she hoped that this house was the answer to her prayers. Finally, her days would be filled with the elusive elation everyone around her seemed to experience.

"Will it?" She wrapped her hands around her arms and didn't turn. He'd see the tears shining in her eyes and he'd ask questions—about her, about her past—that she wasn't prepared to answer.

"Aye. You can trust an Irishman's word."

She saw his reassuring smile reflected in the glass. The expression in his eyes, though, was a mirror of her own. Intense and probing.

And she knew what it meant.

He was beginning to fall for her, just as she was falling for him.

He turned her around to face him, his hands resting loosely on her shoulders. "I'm here for you, and I won't leave until this renovation is finished."

"Thanks. It's just—" A wave of emotion choked her voice, and she couldn't get out any words. Strange. She never lost control. After she and her sister had been passed from one foster home to another, she'd learned to keep her feelings securely bound. Not a single person was interested in two teenage girls with no money and no skills. No one had wanted them.

Not even their own mother and father had cared—so why would anyone else?

A ripple of sadness caused tears to stream down her cheeks. Swiftly, she caught the wetness with her fingertips and avoided Keiran's gaze.

"You're a nobody." The harsh words of one of her foster mothers came to the forefront of Desiree's mind. In her early teens, arriving at a brand-new foster family's home, Desiree had broken a dish by mistake. She'd tried to be useful, drying the dishes. Her foster mother had been furious, reprimanding Desiree about having no respect for other people's things, and shouting that Desiree was a useless girl.

Desiree had cried herself to sleep that night. She remembered the loneliness, the sadness, the sense of never belonging. Feasibly, that was the reason she felt inept in the kitchen.

Keiran watched her closely. He seemed unsure what to say next.

Lightly, he kneaded her shoulders. "Are you okay?" he asked quietly.

Grateful, she accepted his silent comfort, his reassuring presence.

"Of course," she murmured. She averted her gaze and thrust her fingers through her hair, attempting to right her curls into a semblance of order. She hadn't bothered to run a comb through her tangles since she'd gotten home, and probably looked a mess.

I'm not a nobody, she reminded herself. *Lift your chin and compose your features. 'Unsophisticated' and 'unimportant' do not belong in your vocabulary anymore. You're a poised, professional, educated woman.*

Although sometimes, oftentimes—she attempted to convince herself more than anyone else.

Gradually, she realized that Keiran was still staring at her, still had his hands on her shoulders.

She raised her gaze to meet his. "What's the matter?" she asked.

"Nothing." He cleared his throat, his face so near that his clear green eyes reminded her of Irish shamrocks, vivid and vital. "I was thinking that I debated about coming back to Roses and starting over. When I first arrived in Atlanta ten years ago, I assumed I was going to live there forever. And now I'm glad—"

Her heart responded in a slow, steady beat. "Glad about what?"

"And now I'm glad I came back. If I hadn't, I wouldn't have met you."

"I'm glad you came too." He was so close she could feel his sweet breath on her cheek. "I would have spent the week trying to find firewood to keep this fireplace burning."

Clearly amused, he said, "I assume you found enough wood."

"Yes, I brought in a few logs the other night, remember? You had stacked a cord behind the fence."

He didn't respond at first. His amusement was replaced by a slow, simmering intensity.

"So you found the firewood." He lowered his head, his lips meeting hers. "And I found you."

CHAPTER 5

Another week went by, marking the fourteenth day until Christmas.

On Friday evening, Keiran experimented with a new dish, mushroom stroganoff, which delighted Desiree. It was heartening to have a simple, unpretentious meal waiting for her when she came home after an exhausting workday.

Following the meal and clean-up, he shadowed her into the living room carrying two glasses of sparkling cider, plates of another Irish whiskey cake he'd baked, and napkins. He stacked kindling over crumpled newspaper in the fireplace, lit the newspaper first, then added large logs. Satisfied, he took a seat beside her on her gray-fabric sofa.

She gazed at the ten-foot spruce tree he'd purchased. Placed in a corner of the large room, the forest-green pine made a majestic statement.

After visiting several Christmas tree sites the previous weekend, Keiran had maintained that the largest tree on the lot was the ideal size to complement her living room's grand design. The tree seller had assisted Keiran in securing the tree to the roof of his truck, and Keiran had driven back to her house slowly with the tree swinging precariously on top.

Between making creamy eggnog and cranking up Yuletide music on a holiday radio station, Desiree and Keiran had decided on traditional red and green lights and a dazzling angel tree topper. Desiree had insisted on sparkly silver tinsel and a popcorn garland, and Keiran had enhanced the glittery embellishments with an array of wooden toy soldier ornaments he'd carved. The result was vibrant, festive, and in Keiran's words, "a masterpiece."

"I might pick up another tree," he casually said.

"One isn't enough? Completely decorated, this tree is practically taking up half my living room."

He grinned impishly, highlighting his boyish features. "I'd like to sprinkle Christmas all through the house. A small tree for the dining room would look festive."

"Especially because I don't own a dining room table or chairs." Desiree picked up the two glasses of sparkling cider from the end table beside her, handed one to him, and beckoned to the fireplace. "You know, everyone at my law firm is encouraging me to convert my fireplace to gas."

"It's your house and you've worked hard to acquire it. You should do what you want." His encouragement was gracious, and a surge of happiness flowed through her that had nothing to do with the delicious meal, the enchantment of a heartening fire on a cold winter's night, or the approaching holidays.

It was him. It was Keiran.

Seeing him like this, relaxed, wearing dark-wash jeans and a sea-green sweater that hugged his wide shoulders to perfection, he lounged beside her on her ten-year-old sofa. How could she remain unaffected when he was so breathtakingly handsome?

"Yes, this house is mine, and I still can't believe it," she replied. "And . . ." She hesitated, trying not to get ahead of herself. This was just the beginning. This was just a house. He was just a man she loved spending every waking hour with.

Just a man.

"And what?" He sipped his cider, set it on the coffee table, and moved nearer. His male presence was compelling, and a quiver of attraction went through her.

Quickly, she pushed the thoughts away, attempting a composure she didn't quite feel.

"I love the smell of a woodburning fireplace, so I'm passing on the gas insert," she said. "Call me outdated."

He pressed a soft kiss to her cheek and murmured agreement.

She gave him a questioning glance. "Can I ask you something?"

"Sure."

"Why did you leave Roses? You had the world at your feet."

"Did I? Tell that to an impulsive teenager." He reached for his glass and drained the cider. "I'll give you the short version, and please don't be sympathetic."

"And if I am?"

He hesitated, his features unreadable. "Don't be."

"Is my question too personal?"

He gave her a look that said it wasn't. "My father and I didn't agree about what I wanted to do for a living," Keiran said. "So, being reckless and headstrong, I decided my way was best."

"Which was?"

"Moving to Atlanta. I planned to become tops in my profession."

"Doing what?"

"Opening my own restaurant."

"And what was your father's way?"

"He wanted me to become an NFL football player. Trouble is, I didn't have the drive, or the interest, or the talent. I was the tallest on the team, but certainly not the fastest."

"I remember seeing you in your football uniform at the homecoming game I attended," she said. "It was the first time I ever saw you."

He offered an indifferent shrug. "Did you actually watch the game?"

"A little, I think. I don't remember you on the playing field."

"You have an awesome memory."

"Why?"

He hesitated. Her question sat in the space between them.

"Because I hardly ever played and frankly, I was relieved, although I knew my father was disappointed." Regret shadowed Keiran's gaze. "The football coach put me on the team to please my father because our pub was one of the sponsors. Soon after that game, I quit."

"I caught glimpses of you in the high school halls. Quitting didn't seem to affect your popularity."

A statement, not a question.

"I suppose." He shrugged. "Although popularity is a difficult word to define, especially when it's used to categorize people."

Wistfully, she gazed at the twinkling tree lights, the shades of red and green belonging to a simpler time, offset by the muted tones of the rustic toy soldiers. Could Christmas be celebrated without glossy bulbs and the sophisticated backdrop of her living room?

Of course.

As a child, well, she had certainly longed for Christmas, although it had never been celebrated at her house. Beer cans littered the floor and food was scarce. Christmas was a luxury her parents couldn't afford, and Santa Claus had never visited.

As an adult, she couldn't imagine life without Christmas. She loved the gift-giving and feasting, the religious celebration, the sacredness of the special holiday.

Profoundly moved by a feeling she couldn't explain, she blinked as her vision blurred. "In my childhood, I wanted a real home so badly—the picket fence, a cute puppy sitting by a welcoming fire burning in the grate, surrounded by people who loved me. When my mother was well and not drinking, she said she envisioned herself as a grand lady living on a beautiful estate." Desiree's lungs and throat felt sore, and she swallowed. "Considering our two-room shack, my mother had quite the imagination."

Tears pricked Desiree's eyes and she wiped them away. She scolded herself for dredging up emotional memories, better kept sealed in a safe corner of her mind. Inhaling, she sat erect. "So what you're saying is that at the end of your senior year, you took off because you didn't get the opportunity to play on the high school team?"

"C'mon, Desiree. Do I seem as shallow as all that? I said I quit football."

"Sorry." She paused. "I mean, you lived in one of the most expensive communities in Roses. I would have given the world to grow up in your shoes."

"It's never just about the stunning home and expensive neighborhood," he said softly. "There's more to a person's story than what's on the surface. I went to Atlanta to pursue my dream, got sidetracked, and failed."

Desiree tipped her face back to view him. He expected to see disapproval on her beautiful features. After all, he'd had everything and given it all up, while she'd had nothing.

"You're young and can achieve anything you want." A positive smile played on her lips. "Also, you're one of the most talented people I've ever met. But look, we can talk about something else if you're uncomfortable."

"I don't mind our discussion, Desiree." He nodded his assent.

He'd been undecided about what to say, about his past, his future, although being with her lightened his concerns. With Desiree, everything would be okay.

He realized she was watching him, apparently waiting for him to continue.

He put his hands on his knees and focused on the wood sparking in the fireplace, the frosted pine cones and garland adorning the wide wooden mantel. The stylish adornments gave the room a celebratory spirit.

"My father discouraged me from what I wanted to do with my life," he said. "I intended to own a restaurant. Therefore, I rebelled."

"And here I thought you wanted to be a carpenter," she teased.

He pushed out a sigh. "I like woodworking, although my passion is the restaurant business. It's how I grew up. I love the hustle and bustle, the busy dinner hours, the scents of shepherd's pie, potato and leek soup, and thyme complementing my parents' famous corned beef recipe."

She gazed at him, openly interested. "I'm surprised."

"Mind if I ask why?"

Her unpretentious warmth set her apart from any woman he'd ever known. Was that what captivated him about her? Besides her vivaciousness, her sensational figure, and her utterly polished appearance when she came home each evening.

That is, until she pulled her hair from her severe bun and let the blond waves fall down her back. Then she looked irresistible.

She studied his face with a concerned frown. "Because most parents would have been thrilled their kid wanted to follow in their footsteps."

"Mine weren't. They insisted that owning an eating establishment was too difficult because of the long hours, which included early mornings, late evenings, and most holidays." He forked a corner of cake on his plate and chewed around the lump in his throat. "Did you know only one third of all restaurants succeed?"

"I've heard it's one in ten."

He paused, forming his words while he stared at the pile of sheetrock marking the next space in her home to be renovated—the small study attached to the living room via French doors.

"Living in Roses, you probably heard talk that my parents lived beyond their means," he said. "At first they did well and their pub was a huge success. Sadly, they didn't plan for the lean years."

"Yes. I heard." Despite her polite nod, he could tell she knew more than she let on. It was no secret his parents had neglected the pub after his departure, eventually forcing it to close. Even their most loyal customers could no longer endure the erratic schedule and so-so meals.

"They moved to Ireland soon afterward. Dublin," he clarified, briefly closing his eyes. "Although they reached out to me, I never flew across the pond to see them except to attend their funerals years later. They died within a day of each other. In the end, discouragement broke their hearts."

"Keiran."

He opened his eyes. Her gaze held his.

"I'm genuinely sorry. You realize none of this is your fault," she said. "My parents died while serving sentences for several robberies. They were alcoholics."

He felt a twist of sadness in his gut. For her. For him.

She was so sweet, so vulnerable, so totally gorgeous, he was torn between kissing her and commiserating on their losses.

He decided on the latter, and enfolded her into his arms.

Would kissing her mess things up? They got along brilliantly, although he often felt off balance. Could they keep their relationship casual, yet professional, living under the same roof, coming to terms with their attraction? His thoughts scattered, although he already knew the answer.

Nope.

With Desiree, his feelings were too deep to be casual.

He gazed at her mouth and cupped her chin in his hands, forcing her to gaze at him.

What would it be like to kiss her again and again?

Nope, his conscience chimed in a second time. She'd made her intentions known without saying a word. This was a business relationship.

Then why did life with her seem spot-on? Was the universe telling him something—bringing him back to Roses after all this time to open a pub, and bringing him to her? He was at the tail end of one profession, embarking on another. And she was the bridge in between. Or was she more? Perhaps she was the missing link . . . the real reason he was here.

She drew a sharp breath. "Keiran, I—"

He lowered his head and brushed his lips against hers. If she rejected him, he'd deal with it.

She didn't.

With a whisper of acquiescence, she twined her hands around his neck and pressed her delicate body closer.

He shivered. “Do you know how many times I’ve wanted to kiss you these past two weeks?” His hands slid down her back. “I mean, really kiss you?”

“Then what were you waiting for?” came her teasing reply.

He hadn’t planned to spend Friday evening kissing her, he told his intrusive conscience. He’d planned on conversing with her, bantering with her, comparing recipes and paint samples.

Or had he? Because devoting every minute of his free time to her felt like the most natural thing in the world.

Slowly, tenderly, he took her lips in a lingering, passionate kiss.

Her cell phone chirped.

She always had it near in case one of her clients experienced a family emergency. For a second, she hesitated, then drew away from him. She picked up her phone and read the screen. “It’s Candee,” she said. “She and Teddy and Joseph want to stop over. Candee is helping me plan my Christmas Eve dinner menu.”

“Tonight? Christmas isn’t for a while yet.” Keiran couldn’t hide his disappointment. He wanted to spend the evening alone with Desiree. “When? If they’ve started walking, they’ll be here in two minutes.”

“They’re still at their house.” Desiree tapped a text on her phone. “I’ll tell her tomorrow is better. Besides, I’m electing you as head preparer for Christmas Eve dinner. You’re much better suited to the task, so you should be the one to talk with her.”

He brought Desiree back into his arms, fingering the lustrous texture of her hair, breathing in the scent of vanilla and a fresh winter breeze.

"If you'd like," he said, "I'll teach you everything I know."

"Didn't you already offer me that once? Umm, no thanks. You know way too much about too many things—carpentry, decorating, football—"

He laughed. "I'm hardly an expert on anything, especially football."

Her gorgeous eyes sparkled. "Keiran, I hear you play your guitar every night when I'm in bed. You're also an excellent musician."

He'd forgotten her bedroom was directly below his attic apartment. "Do I disturb you?"

"On the contrary. You play really well."

He placed his hand along the curve of her velvety cheek. "Shall I serenade you sometime, my stunning Queen Anne?"

"You sound like a chivalrous knight, although I'm no queen." She grinned. "You're confusing *me* with my Queen-Anne style *home*."

"You're not a queen?" In exaggerated surprise, he splayed his fingers across his chest.

She laughed. "The bay window and spindle work in my home are—"

"Exquisite. Just like you."

"Hardly." The color rose in her cheeks. She didn't meet his gaze, instead looking toward the wavy glass windowpanes splattered with rain. "Most people define me as a workaholic."

"There's nothing wrong with being a workaholic. I prefer the term 'overachiever,' which is an admirable trait."

She shifted and pulled her blue cardigan closer around her shoulders. "Oftentimes, my work gets in the way of the important things in my life—family, friends, and good times."

"I've been accused of the same."

She nodded, agreeing. "I've always believed my career

came first. I've analyzed myself because I've read that understanding the problem is the best way to heal."

"Overachieving isn't a problem, Desiree."

"In some ways it is." Her smooth forehead knit into a pensive frown. "Candee and I have discussed our childhood. More often than not, we were neglected and now we're trying to compensate."

"By buying dilapidated houses?"

"It seems like that, doesn't it?"

"A little." He tried to think of words to encourage her, because he was picturing her as a young girl with fine blond hair and delicate features, helpless and alone. He realized he hadn't spoken for several moments and reminded himself to keep the conversation going. "And what else did your discussion with your sister uncover?" he asked.

Desiree slumped against the couch. "We were parentless children, raising ourselves the best we knew how."

"You had a mother and father."

"They were absent even when they were around. And the parent-child roles were reversed. Candee and I took care of them."

Gently, he slid his arm around her shoulders. "Candee and I spoke one afternoon, and she mentioned your last set of foster parents became your forever family."

"Yes, they're good people." The pensiveness in Desiree's gaze stirred his heart. "They love Candee and me, and email us regularly since they moved away. I'm grateful they came into our lives and offered love and stability."

But still.

She didn't say it, despite the words hanging in the air. She was trying to make up for the negligence in her childhood by . . . by what? Overachieving?

Something about the desolation on her face made him want to do whatever possible to shape her world for the better. She had a successful career, a lovely home, a caring sister.

And she had his heart.

He paused.

His heart?

Aye—and the realization took a firm place in his gut. He'd been half in love with her since the first day they'd met and she'd slammed the front door in his face, then teased him about talking to her porch.

With great effort, he stopped himself from repeating his thoughts aloud, although the shout-in-his-face awareness of their chemistry made him catch his breath. He liked being with her, conversing and comforting her.

No, it was too soon. He wasn't seeking a romance after his breakup with Patricia.

Better to keep things light. Besides, he didn't plan on staying in Desiree's home much longer. As soon as the holidays were over and her house was in better order, he planned to rent an apartment in town.

Move on.

But now, things were different. Fixing her home, spending memorable evenings beside her, anticipating the joyous holiday, and yes, discussing their childhoods—with all the hurts, all the dreams—was the most natural thing in the world. They were content, and he felt as if he'd known her his entire life. She'd given him a peephole into her past, and he'd done the same.

He cradled her face between his fingers, stroking an errant tear from her cheek.

"I'm grateful you came into my life. Or rather, I'm grateful I came into yours."

The tenderness in her soft eyes and lips tore down his defenses. She sparked a yearning in him he barely recognized, reminding him that there was more to life than successful pubs and impeccable carpentry. And these feelings were new. Not even with Patricia had he felt this utter sense of fulfillment.

His mouth descended on hers. She followed his lead, sliding her hands down his shoulders. Her lips were warm and smooth as velvet, tasting of sweet caramel and Irish whiskey cake.

He told himself to go slowly. His lips said otherwise. Their breaths heated the air around them.

An eternity later, the kiss ended.

As they gazed at each other, longing shown from her intense blue eyes.

Along with another emotion.

Wariness?

"You are beautiful," he whispered. "And that was—" How could he find a phrase to describe it?

"Not a good idea," she said.

"You're kidding!" He jerked his head back. "That's what you were thinking?"

"Keiran, we have a business arrangement. Anything else will only complicate things."

He was still searching for an accurate description of their kiss, while she was headed to the other side of the couch.

As usual, she was spot on. They'd only just met.

"Then will you go on a date with me?" he asked.

"After what I just said?"

"I understand you want to take our relationship slowly and I respect your wishes. Let's start with a real date."

She moistened her lips, just enough to captivate him. "A date where? To the kitchen?"

"I was thinking somewhere a little farther." He laughed. "Lunch or dinner in one of the town's restaurants?" His plan was to get to know her. Sure, he was living in her house and familiar with her daily routine, but it wasn't enough. He wanted to learn more.

She spoke what was on her mind, and she was interesting to be around. She was a brave woman. A Christian possessing a kind spirit. Strong, yet gentle. Courageous, yet yielding. Open, yet unassuming.

And these attributes fascinated him.

"Will you play your guitar for me?" she asked.

He widened his eyes at the unexpected question. "Maybe later," he said.

She granted him an audacious smile. "Please, Keiran?"

He knew he could never deny her anything.

Within minutes, he tromped to the attic and reappeared with his father's acoustic guitar. He tuned the strings and strummed a few chords. "What do you want to hear?"

She sat erect, glancing at him, then his guitar. "Something Christmassy."

He plucked the melody of "Jingle Bells" while she sang the lyrics, her voice light and in tune.

When he finished the final refrain, he broke into the beginning of "Don't Stop Believin'."

"That's the song you play in the attic," she said. "I couldn't place the group."

"Journey," he supplied. "Often, my father played the piece after our pub closed for the evening. My mother used to complain it was the only song he knew."

"I read somewhere the composer of that song was inspired by his father's words of encouragement."

"Aye, and the song held special significance for my father, also," Keiran said. "He came to this town disillusioned after he wasn't picked in the NFL draft, and rose to success when he met my mother and they opened the pub. Sadly, the pub closed when he ran out of funds."

"Why, when the pub was so popular at first?" Waiting, she

surveyed him, giving him the kindhearted expression he was coming to know so well.

"Maybe because all along my father was disheartened. Although he worked hard, his initial dreams of becoming a professional football player didn't pan out," Keiran said. "And then, of course, I left."

He shifted, silent for a beat.

"Did this guitar belong to your father?" Desiree asked, breaking the silence.

"Aye. He bequeathed it to me in his will. This and his abandoned Irish pub in town."

"So you own O'Malley's?"

"There's nothing to own. It's my father's broken legacy. This beat-up guitar, an abandoned pub, and a trading card autographed by a famous football player my father met while he was training."

"Hold on. Is the card worth anything?"

"I checked a few years ago because my former roommate, Georges, works at a pawn shop in Atlanta. The card is a 1976 Topps card, and the player didn't sign many, so the estimated worth is around fifteen thousand dollars."

"Certainly, it's a card to treasure and hold on to."

"And it brings back memories, both good and bad." Keiran released a deep breath and set the guitar to the side. "When I attended my parents' funerals in Dublin, I'm ashamed to tell you I was angry and bitter. My cousin William reassured me that although I wasn't there for them, they were always in my heart."

She squeezed his hand. "I know."

"I didn't walk away from my parents because I didn't care. I walked away because I didn't know if I had it in me to live up to my father's expectations. I knew I couldn't be a pro football player, so I disengaged. I found myself in a state of panic."

Caught in the spell of her captivating blue eyes, he placed his arm around her shoulders.

"Go on," she prompted. "You mentioned your cousin William."

He didn't want to spoil their evening by speaking about sadness. Attempting to recover their former gaiety, he replied with an expressive beam. "William lives in Ireland and has the proverbial Irish philosophy. He connects with people and believes forgiveness is most important. It's called Irish craic."

Desiree shot him a quizzical look. "I'm not following."

"Irish craic is fun and good times. William is humorous and witty and earnestly interested in others. You'll like him."

"I'll like him . . . when? I've never visited Ireland nor do I plan to in the future."

"Someday."

Silence lingered between them.

"With my investment in this house, an overseas trip isn't possible," she quietly replied.

"Never say never," Keiran advised. "My father threatened he wouldn't take me back if I ever appeared in Roses again. And here I am, not certain if I'm moving forward or backward, only knowing I was wrong to leave in the first place."

"Don't feel guilty." She touched his arm. "That's life, isn't it? We make mistakes, we brush ourselves off, and we go on."

"Do we ever forgive ourselves?" His voice came as a whisper.

"It's Christmas, the season of forgiveness," she said. "And the answer is an emphatic yes."

CHAPTER 6

"Tomorrow is the bake-off contest," Keiran reminded Desiree as she entered the foyer.

"It's written in bold on my calendar." Desiree set down her briefcase and joked, "How could I ever forget?"

Finally, it was Friday, the last day of another grueling work week.

"I'm glad to see you, gorgeous." He helped her off with her sunny-yellow raincoat and took her in his arms for a long kiss.

He'd been waiting for her at the foot of the stairs, the sparse lighting glinting over his hair. Thick, wavy, and midnight-black. And he looked oh so incredibly handsome.

He was dressed in a cotton chambray shirt unbuttoned at the neckline, showing a deep vee at his throat. His denims were well fitted. Tall, well-built, and confident, he sent her pulse racing. His physique would stop any woman in her tracks.

She linked her fingers around his nape, thinking all the while that he was the type of man she could easily fall in love with.

Wow. Whoa.

Love was the doorway to sorrow, and she'd had enough disappointment to know better than to risk her heart again.

Still, Keiran might be worth the risk. It was pure bliss having his strong, secure arms around her. Love was a quiet, joyous peace with no barriers. Love was exactly that with this man.

For an instant, she squeezed her eyes closed. *No. No. No.*

As much as she cared for him, they could never be together. Although he was talented and creative, he hadn't decided on a career for himself. Cooking or carpentry?

After her chaotic childhood, she knew stability was her primary goal.

Her feelings warred ferociously, and she considered telling him how much she cared, and what she most feared if they were to go forward in their relationship—that he could easily pick up and leave at any time.

Stability. Stability.

Numbly, she pulled from his arms.

He watched her, his gaze penetrating. He was always in tune with her emotions. "Is everything okay?"

"Of course." She dragged her gaze from his and focused on the authentic tin ceiling tile he'd replaced in the foyer. The edges were trimmed neatly and seamlessly overlapped.

Before she could remark on his excellent workmanship, he brushed a kiss across her temple. "Are you ready for an amazing time tomorrow, gorgeous?"

Gorgeous. No one had ever called her gorgeous. Profoundly touched, she brushed away a tear before his perceptive green-eyed gaze leveled on her. She wasn't used to praises, to his unbending good nature, and didn't know how to react.

"I'm ready to win the cake contest." She gave him her best challenging gaze while she shook lingering droplets from her black pencil skirt. Raindrops had chased each other across her car's windshield all the way home. If only it would snow to complete the holiday season.

"We'll see about that." He hung her raincoat in the foyer closet, then laid a callused hand on her cheek. His touch was reassuring. "So how was your day?"

"Demanding, as usual." Without prompting, she lifted her face for a kiss. "I'm delighted I only have one more work week to go before Christmas. You?"

"Hectic. The study off the living room has been sheetrocked and sanded, and the guys left some of their tools there. All you have to do is choose a paint color."

"My specialty."

"That's my girl." He grinned, drawing her to him. "Desiree, I have a confession."

The way he said her name, low and husky, resembled a loving caress.

Her gaze narrowed on his grin. "What is it?" That feeling, that draw, grew stronger each time they were together. That little flip of exhilaration.

"For the first time in a long time, I'm anticipating an amazing holiday." The sentiment in his voice melted her heart. "And it's all because of you."

"I am too." She was helpless to resist him, moving automatically into his arms. "And I'm glad to be home."

"To see me," he clarified.

"Indeed."

"Did you think about me today?"

"Often," she admitted. *Very often.*

"Good. I thought about you too. See how much we are alike? We both love Christmas and we both love—" He bent his head and kissed her deeply, thoroughly.

Both love what?

Each other?

She'd spent far too long trying to figure out men and relationships, and reveled in his kisses instead. She couldn't pull away from him even if she wanted to.

Excuse me, her conscience kicked in. *You're losing your focus.*

Yes, well, because around him she could hardly think. She wasn't good at this—dating—the entire courting process. Her career had always been most important.

Now she wished for more, wished for him.

He'd never mentioned a girlfriend, dismissing Desiree's inquiry with a wave of his hand. He'd explained that he'd dated in Atlanta, although no one worth mentioning. She'd been relieved he hadn't had a serious affair of the heart, although she'd told him about Scott, her ex. She hadn't said much, but apparently just enough, because Keiran had remarked he was sorry she'd been hurt.

His lips twitched as he drew her closer. "I'm glad you're glad to see me."

"Is that proper English?"

His lips moved within an inch of hers. "It is now."

She felt her cheeks flush as she gazed at his ruggedly handsome face.

"Who is judging our cakes?" she asked.

"Excellent change of subject. What cakes?" Smirking, he took her hand and led her to the kitchen. "First, have a cuppa tea with me. I brewed loose leaf tea using a strainer." He pulled out a stool for her, then poured her a steaming cup. "Sugar? Milk?"

"No thanks." She savored a swallow. Loose leaf tea was definitely more flavorful than tea bags. Again, she asked, "So, who is judging our cakes?"

"Several ladies on the town board, and some guy named Rob who owns a chain of bakeries in Florida," Keiran said.

She gasped and set down her cup. "Rob, as in Rob's Marvelous Muffins?"

"Aye." Keiran claimed the seat across from her. "Is he famous or something?"

"He certainly is famous, at least in Miami." Desiree rested her elbows on the island. "Rob is Teddy's mentor and a good friend. He lent Teddy the money for his start-up real estate business. Rob wants to expand his bakeries to another state and is considering Roses because Teddy and Candee are here."

The subject came up again an hour later, after they'd dined on a savory beef and Guinness stew brimming with carrots, potatoes, onions, and chunks of beef.

"I met him when Teddy and Candee got married." Desiree scraped plates while Keiran loaded the dishwasher. "Rob is great fun. You'll like him. Plus, you're both restauranteurs." She paused. "Is that a word?"

An amused gleam lit Keiran's eyes. "Absolutely, and it means the owner or manager of a restaurant. Although technically, I never owned a restaurant. My parents owned the pub."

"Same difference. And you own the pub now."

"True."

She finished wiping down the kitchen counter. "Who else is participating in the baking contest?"

"It's open to everyone. From what I gather, the town will set up tables for our cakes and an awning is being erected in case of bad weather." A lazy smile graced his face. "By the way, Candee is baking a Christmas cake."

"She's participating? To my knowledge, she's never turned on an oven in her life."

"The cake is a surprise. Or rather, it was a surprise until I spilled the beans." A sheepish grin crossed his lips as he gave an apologetic shrug. "Rob flew in from Miami and is staying with Candee and Teddy. Word is that Rob is baking the cake."

Desiree's competitive spirit jumped into true form. "So I'm competing against Rob, who bakes for a living, and you, the guy who's been basting an Irish whiskey cake for four days?"

He chuckled. "The odds are in your favor, though."

"How?"

"You're the prettiest." He stepped behind her and wrapped his arms around her waist. Nuzzling his lips against her neck, he murmured, "Are you certain you have to work next week?"

"Yes, if you want to get paid."

"I work for next to nothing," he joked. "I want a raise."

She laughed, shook her head, and tugged from his grasp. "Not happening."

That morning, she'd driven with a smile on her face all the way to her law firm in the middle of town. Keiran's parents' pub, O'Malley's, was located a few blocks away. Years earlier, the building had been abandoned and boarded up. A "For Lease" sign had hung on the door for ages.

As she'd walked from her car to her office, she'd tried to stop thinking about Keiran.

The more she'd tried, the more she'd failed. And now, another week had passed and Christmas was closing in. So much had happened since he'd arrived. And it was all good. So, so good.

He was a miracle worker, transforming her home into an enchanting, welcoming place. He spent hours in the kitchen after Teddy's crew knocked off for the day, and often sent Candee his baked goods, which she, Teddy, and Joseph enthusiastically praised.

Each evening, Desiree finished her last client's filing with an eye on the clock, counting the minutes until she could see Keiran.

And tomorrow, a week before Christmas, she and Keiran were participating in a baking contest.

She shook her head and added a grin. Her dashing Irishman, her one-of-a-kind Renaissance man, was as equally at home measuring and marking drywall as he was experimenting with a new recipe, or strumming a melody on his guitar.

She closed her eyes and thanked God. During the most blessed season of the year, when she was worried and despondent, He had brought Keiran into her life.

Certainly, she had much to be thankful for. She was no longer stuck in a bad situation with an ex who didn't care about her.

Have faith, her chaplain had preached numerous times.

But how?

She had wondered—as an orphaned teen, as a grown woman with a broken heart.

God had seemed invisible, but He hadn't been. He'd been working for her good all along.

* * *

THE FOLLOWING morning dawned bright and chilly, and sunlight shone through the wavy glass bay window in the living room.

Keiran and Desiree relished their first cup of coffee for the day. Even when their mornings began before dawn, he brewed a fresh pot of coffee and prepared a hearty cooked breakfast. He loved cooking for her.

"You're staring at me again," Desiree said.

"Am I?" He set down his cup. "I can't help it. You're gorgeous." That figure, dressed in flattering faux-leather leggings, suede ankle boots, and a creamy tweed sweater. And those cornflower-blue eyes, even more fascinating than her legs.

Delight quickened inside him. He'd come to Roses to pick up what he'd abandoned ten years before. A timeworn pub. He'd assumed he'd go it alone, far from Atlanta and Patricia.

Except he wasn't alone anymore.

With Desiree, he instinctively felt a sense of coming home and knew that embarking on this journey without her was unthinkable.

He openly admired her as she picked up their empty cups. Her beauty was stunning.

"I'll finish clearing," he offered, coming to his feet.

She held up a hand. "Keiran, I may not be the world's greatest cook, but I certainly know how to keep things tidy. Please let me do a little something to repay all you've done."

"Okay." His gaze shifted to those figure-hugging leggings before doubling back to her face.

She regarded him with her lovely, shiny eyes and smiled.

He thought about her throughout his day while he multi-tasked, installing molding, cutting and sawing wood, and picking up debris after the other crews clocked out.

She'd asked him once if he ever slept, and he'd teased that he obviously didn't require as much sleep as she did.

"Ready for the contest?" he asked, following her to the kitchen where their cakes sat on the counter.

"I feel anything but ready." She set her coffee cup in the sink. "Otherwise, yes, sure."

He helped her on with her cobalt-blue coat. She'd worn her blond hair loose, and she ran her fingers through the ends in that graceful, unassuming way of hers.

They placed their finished cakes on cake boards, then packed them in sturdy, clean covered boxes.

Desiree insisted on them both driving their vehicles to

the event, as she had to pick up a bag of groceries at her favorite green grocer when they were finished. He drove behind her car and parked in an empty parking space. As they got out of their vehicles, Desiree remarked that she felt motivated by seeing all the small-town celebrations.

Her pistachio cake, garnished with powdered sugar and maraschino cherries, presented an eye-catching display. Although Keiran's Irish whiskey cake didn't appear as vibrant, his baking process had taken longer. He'd carefully wrapped the cake, refrigerated it for three days and added a glaze on the fourth.

The first prize for the event was an apron, stamped with a red and green *Kiss Me, It's Christmas* motif.

He and Desiree set their cakes on a long table beneath an expansive white canvas awning on the green. The judges provided cake stands that elevated the cakes to a magnificent new level.

"I'll be wearing that apron when I cook the Christmas Eve dinner you volunteered me to prepare," Keiran baited.

He expected a teasing rejoinder, and she didn't disappoint.

She leaned toward him and joked, "You'll be wearing that apron because I let you *borrow* it. And don't forget we eat dinner at six o'clock sharp."

He gave a shout of laughter as they wended through the crowd and perused the food kiosks. Near the judges' stand she halted in midstep. Spotting Candee and Teddy, Desiree took hold of Keiran's hand and rushed over to them.

As planned, Candee and Teddy were manning a booth distributing free hot chocolate and candy canes to the participants and attendees. Nearby, Joseph skipped and played tag in an adjacent play area with a couple of new friends.

Teddy had confided to Keiran that the boy had changed

significantly since moving to Roses. His demeanor was perky, his gaze gleaming with delight.

"Uncle Teddy, watch me!" the boy called. He'd settled down to working with his playmates to build a sandcastle in the sandbox.

"There's Rob." Desiree waved gaily to an older, bald-headed man, then brought Keiran over to meet him.

"Hello, I'm Keiran O'Malley, Desiree's carpenter." Keiran extended his hand as they met. "I've heard a lot about you."

"I'm Rob the baker." The man beamed good-naturedly. "Although you've got me beat because you're the baker *and* the carpenter. Do you also make candles?"

Keiran blinked.

"You know, the butcher, the baker, and the candlestick—" Rob laughed heartily, gripped Keiran's hand, and vigorously shook it. "An old nursery rhyme. Mother Goose and what-not. Never mind. You're too young for rhymes, and I'm too old to be able to recite them correctly."

Keiran nodded. What was Rob getting at? "Sorry, I'm not following."

He glanced at Desiree, who grinned and shrugged. "Rob's not talking about nursery rhymes," she said. "He means—"

"I've heard about your baking and carpentry skills, Keiran," Rob interrupted. "Teddy expounded at length. You're good at one, exceptional at the other."

"That's a fair assessment," Keiran replied. "Should I ask which one is better?"

Rob checked out Keiran's Irish whiskey cake, set on a white platter and topped with spiced chopped pecans. "Your baking won by a landslide. Can you cook too?"

"Lots of down-home food including corned beef and cabbage and shepherd's pie. Although I like experimenting with new recipes, Guinness stew is my specialty."

"I can attest to that," Desiree said with a Mona Lisa smile.

"Excellent. You can experiment on me anytime. I told Teddy I was going on a diet." Rob patted his protruding stomach. "Though I've decided to wait until the New Year. Maybe my local gym will have a special."

Keiran laughed. He liked Rob's responses. He was a good, honest guy. "My parents owned a pub in town. They served authentic Irish food and homemade desserts."

"Oh?" Rob gave the surrounding streets a once-over. "Which one?"

"Walking distance from here. The pub's been empty a long time, although it was once busy with customers lining up outside the door when we opened for the day."

As Keiran pointed in the pub's direction, Desiree and Rob followed his gaze.

"Is the place available for rent?" Rob asked.

Desiree placed a hand on Keiran's arm. "The pub's been boarded up for years, although Keiran inherited it from his parents."

Keiran shifted. She was telling Rob more than he needed to know.

He and Desiree had visited the pub a few days earlier. Peering through grimy windows, he'd been anxious to assess the place when he'd first arrived, although he'd delayed seeing it, wanting to view the property with her, hesitant about coming to grips with the fact that his parents were no longer alive.

With a tight throat, he'd asked Candee, who was a realtor, to install new door locks. The permit had been provided to him, as the owner, when his parents had passed away. Because the pub was historically significant to the town, O'Malley's had been grandfathered in.

As he'd feared, memories had assailed him when he'd stepped inside—the sticky spilled beer beneath his boots, the heady smell of buttery Irish scones, the pennants from the local sports teams hanging on the timbered walls.

The charm and character of a timeless design.

And he was overwhelmed by his emotions—regret, sadness. And aye, excitement.

Fear of failure, fear of not trying. Was he capable of upholding the legacy of his parents' beloved pub?

Although he didn't have enough capital, should he dare hope he could reopen it? The huge project entailed purchasing inventory, cleaning the place, and passing inspections. Since working for Desiree, he'd saved most of his weekly salary. He'd said goodbye to Atlanta with limited funds, anxious to get away from Patricia.

His Atlanta pastor had once said that if you've gone through a storm, then it was a sure sign that God would be coming. Although Keiran's faith was strong, he'd been skeptical. A storm was difficult. How could it make a person stronger?

More important, was he entitled to success after abandoning his parents? In Roses, in Ireland, they had missed him.

He was selfish. He was undeserving.

He looked past Rob and Desiree. "I own nothing," he said.

"You own a piece of Roses' past." Desiree leaned against him. "Someday, you'll make your pub whole again."

Your pub. *Whole.* Like him, with Desiree by his side.

He knew her well enough to know she'd used the terms on purpose, to give him hope, to support his dream.

"Tell the vendors to start showing up again, and get the word out to former customers that you're planning on reopening," Rob put in. "Then roll up your sleeves and get to work."

Keiran glanced from Rob's firm expression to Desiree's unwavering one.

That day, after viewing the pub, they'd held hands on their way back to his truck.

"I want to make a difference in Roses," he'd said softly.

"So I've heard."

"Once the pub is up and running, I'd like to offer a free meal and worship service every Sunday for the homeless in the community."

"I'll help you." A radiant smile brightened her lovely face as she matched his strong steps. "You're the son who wants to set things right again."

"I feel I must do this."

"Good. This is the place, and this is the time."

The quiet tenderness in her tone was all the reassurance he longed for.

Besides, he loved it here in Roses. The slower pace of life, the sound of children's laughter, the colorful display of twinkling lights around each shop's window.

As Keiran conversed with Rob, gaining insights into running an up-and-coming restaurant, Keiran's questions multiplied.

Desiree gave his hand an encouraging squeeze, excusing herself to go chat with Candee at the hot chocolate stand.

"I have a question," Keiran said to Rob. "Can you guide me?"

"Certainly." Rob's cellphone chirped. "Excuse me. One minute." He held up a hand in apology, pulled out his phone from his colorful plaid jacket, and read the text.

He sent a brief reply. "It's always something in the restaurant business." Rob rolled his eyes and swore under his breath as he clicked off the phone and stuffed it back into his pocket. "One of our customers in Miami complained the service at the bakery was too slow. An employee called in sick and we were short-handed."

"How did you handle it?"

"I'm sending the customer a coupon for a free box of muffins, along with a heartfelt apology. In my opinion, the customer is always right"—he chortled—"even when they aren't."

"Will you hire more employees?" Keiran asked.

"Yes, especially with the busy Christmas season heating up. I own a half-dozen bakeries in the Miami area, so when I think about expanding, I'll employ someone reliable who knows the business." Rob motioned toward Teddy, who was talking with Candee and Desiree while refilling the five-gallon hot chocolate container with water. "I hoped to stay in Roses a couple more days. However, between getting married, formally adopting Joseph, plus renovating his new home, Teddy's got enough to do." He glanced in the direction of the judges' stand. "At any rate, I'll head to Miami tomorrow. What's your question, by the way? Do you need start-up money for your pub?" He dug into his chinos pocket and pulled out his wallet.

"Thank you, but no thank you." Keiran motioned to the wad of hundred-dollar bills Rob extracted, and shook his head.

"Well, from what I hear, you have an excellent work ethic. When the times comes, toss your pride aside and phone me."

"Thanks." Keiran hesitated. "If I ever do, I'll consider it a loan. I'll pay every penny back."

"No worries, as long as your pub becomes a Roses sensation. How's the place looking?"

"Like it's crying out for lots of TLC."

"So, what's your question?" Rob glanced at Desiree, his blue eyes shrewd. "If it concerns a gorgeous blond lawyer who bakes pistachio cakes, then I'm no expert. Inquiries about dating women should be posed to men who have successfully dated them."

"Meaning that, from your experience, women split after the first date?"

"Meaning that, from my experience, women are a full-time job."

"Desiree's not like that." Keiran gazed at her while she and Candee served steaming cups of hot chocolate to a group of teenagers. In the midst of conversation with her sister, she combed the green with her gaze, found him, and gave him a secret smile. He glimpsed the fire smoldering in her eyes and drew a wobbly breath. She was an attraction pulling him to her like a magnet.

Realizing Rob's piercing gaze was fixed on him, Keiran carefully composed his features. "She's brainy and successful and we've become good friends."

"And that's not all." Rob stuffed his wallet back into his pocket and directed a meaningful glance toward her.

"Look, we're taking it slow."

"Uh huh." A skeptical smirk crossed Rob's round face. "Do you want my unasked-for advice?"

Keiran shrugged. "Sure. Why not?"

"If she's anything like her sister Candee, don't let her get away." Rob's smirk widened into a grin. "Besides, I can see that she's already got you smitten. Are you up for the challenge of starting a new life and a new career with a new wife? That's a lot of new."

Rob was dead-on. Aye, Keiran was ready. He embraced challenges and he cared about Desiree. More than cared. He was in love with her. He was in love with her snappy humor, intellect, and especially her openness.

"We'll talk further." Rob hung a left when his name was called at the judging stand. Over his shoulder, he said, "I hope I gave you some food for thought. Get it? Food?" He chuckled at his own joke, then added, "Seriously, I hope I answered your question."

Keiran paused, wondering how he'd started to ask Rob one question—whether Irish whiskey cake could be baked in a jar—and ended up receiving guidance about dating and romance. Although the dating advice Rob had offered was far more significant than a whiskey cake.

Don't let her get away.

Desiree gave Keiran a thoughtful glance as she approached him with two cups of hot chocolate. "Well, you two were deep in conversation."

Keiran accepted a steaming, frothy cup topped with miniature marshmallows. "He's extremely knowledgeable and I'm fortunate to have met him."

"He knows the restaurant business and he can give you lots of excellent tips." She sipped her hot chocolate. "He's a blessing to Teddy and Candee, and stepped in many times to help with Joseph after Teddy's brother Christian died."

"I didn't know."

"The pain of losing Christian was almost Teddy's undoing. Candee helped him begin a new chapter of his life here in Roses."

"Teddy's never talked about it." Keiran was beginning to realize that Desiree's sister and brother-in-law were genuinely good people who cared about others above themselves. He'd also noted the camaraderie between Rob and Teddy as Rob paused in his judging duties to joke with Teddy.

Desiree set her cup down on a tray. "Loss is always hard. Nonetheless, the certainty of a blessed future is guaranteed through faith in God."

With a glance at the holiday festival taking place—the face painter and balloon artist for the children, the four-piece brass band playing Christmas carols—Keiran took heart. Truly, God had brought him to Desiree.

He gazed around, entertained by the small town oozing

with big-time charm. Market stalls along the side streets sold ornaments and nutcrackers, and children mailed their letters to Santa at the corner post office. Historic walking tours were scheduled as soon as the judging finished, and the shops were becoming increasingly crowded with holiday customers.

While a pleasurable morning awaited them, he brought his attention back to the main reason they were here. He slung his arm around Desiree's shoulder and guided her to the colorful array of cakes, lovingly made, and the mouthwatering aromas of butter, sugar, and cherries. The contestants had been instructed to stand behind their respective baked goods to answer questions from the judges.

Delight surged through him. This was perfection. His enchanting birthplace, his exquisite Desiree, and the delight of spending Christmas with her family.

By ten o'clock, the event was finished. Although the contest had been close, the judges announced Desiree had won first place, and Keiran had taken second.

Loud cheering erupted and Desiree blushed gorgeously as a judge tied the red and green *Kiss me, It's Christmas* apron around her cobalt-blue coat. Graciously, she thanked the judges and gave a special mention to Keiran for buying her a kitchen timer.

In a last-minute decision, Candee hadn't entered her Christmas cake. Because Rob had baked it and he was one of the judges, it wouldn't have been fair. Consequently, Rob sat at the judges' stand, along with a plate filled with the cake. At last count, Keiran estimated that Rob had eaten at least three slices, along with a thick wedge of fudge from a food kiosk.

Keiran caught up with Desiree in the middle of the congratulatory crowd. In a laughing voice, she said, "All that powdered sugar paid off."

"Well done." Keiran brought her into his arms for a breathless kiss. Truly, the day couldn't have gone any better.

She hesitated. "You're kissing me here, in front of the entire town?"

"I'm just following directions." He glanced at her apron and grinned.

"It's not Christmas yet."

"I've designated the entire month of December for celebrating Christmas."

Chuckling, she said, "I want to catch up with Candee for a minute."

"Hurry back. There's a Christmassy silk scarf in the front window of one of the boutiques, and I immediately thought of you. You mentioned you wanted a scarf for Christmas."

"I did? When?"

"Well, maybe I just thought you did because I plan to buy it for you."

With a laugh, she pulled off the apron, carefully folded it, then scurried off with it securely tucked under her arm.

Out of the corner of his eye, Keiran noticed Rob speaking to a woman near the judges' stand. Although her back was turned, Keiran felt a wave of familiarity.

The crowd began dispersing and he was facing that same woman a minute later.

A woman he'd assumed he'd never see again. His ex-girlfriend, Patricia.

He gaped. His heartbeat raced.

She stared back at him with a cool smile, her dark hair streaked with blond, and her even white teeth. She was dressed in thigh-high boots, a short pink mini skirt, and a coyote-trimmed puffer jacket. He recognized the expensive jacket, as she'd coveted it the previous year. It had taken all the money he'd set aside, five hundred dollars, but she'd been happy. At least for a little while.

"Patricia?" He said her name and heard the shock in his voice.

"Hi, Keiran. Did you get my text this morning?" Deliberately, she perused Desiree, who'd bounced back to snuggle close to him.

"No. I've been busy," he replied.

He wanted to shout that this was his world, not hers. What was she doing here?

Patricia's gaze slid back to his face. "Well, I arrived."

His stomach plummeted. This couldn't be good. "I see that."

"You two know each other?" Desiree inquired.

Keiran nodded. "Aye," was all he could manage.

"We were practically engaged." Patricia directed her response toward Keiran. "You've been missed."

"Our relationship ended in Atlanta, remember?"

"Maybe our personal relationship." She gave him a heavy stare. "Unfortunately, our business relationship has hit a snag."

Heat flushed through his body. "I left you everything."

Before Patricia could reply, Desiree asked, "Were you two in business together?"

Patricia swept her fingers across Keiran's sleeve, a possessive gesture and decidedly intimate. "He worked for my daddy's company."

The way Patricia had always thrown it up to him twisted Keiran's stomach. In the beginning he had worked for her father, until he'd built his own carpentry business.

"I don't punch a clock for your father anymore," Keiran said.

"True," she rejoined with wry exasperation. "I heard you own a pub in Roses. And I want half the proceeds when you sell." She gestured to the street where O'Malley's was located.

"I'm not selling. And besides, the place hasn't been in business for years."

Her response was a derisive sneer. Few people believed Patricia was anything but a sultry, gorgeous female and ultimate charmer. He knew better. She was a woman who always got what she wanted.

And if she didn't?

Then she'd make life exceedingly unpleasant.

"Everything is for sale for a price." She was talking louder, her shrillness drawing the stares of passing shoppers, as she obviously intended. "Earlier, I went by the pub. It's not worth much, though it's worth something."

He sensed the desperation in her tone and looked her straight in the eye. "So you're here for money?"

"Obviously," she said.

"Where's Kyle?"

"He's long gone."

"And your father?"

"He refused to give me any more money." Her voice lowered to a stage whisper. "Now it's time for you to pay up, Keiran. I get half of everything you earn."

He planned to tread carefully before she went into a fresh fit of anger, although he couldn't contain himself. He just couldn't.

"Our verbal agreement ended." He started to pull his hand away.

"What about our written agreement?" Her grip tightened. Sagely, she shook her head. "You never were good at reading the fine print, darling, were you?"

CHAPTER 7

Laughter burst from the judges' stand, and Desiree jerked at the sound. Keiran shook from Patricia's grip and grabbed Desiree's elbow. He guided her toward the canvas awning, using the excuse he wanted to admire her cake again.

Under her breath, she asked, "What was that about?"

But it didn't matter, because she already knew. And something was shattering deep inside her. Although she tried, she couldn't tear her thoughts away from the lushly provocative Patricia. The woman had the self-confidence of an exceptionally stunning female who commanded attention.

Keiran heaved a sigh. "Her father owns a construction business in Atlanta, and when I met her she got me a job at his company. I learned the trade and became one of his carpentry men."

Desiree felt her face heat, recalling the conversation between Patricia and Keiran. No doubt, they'd been close. Very close. The thought brought a stab of jealousy, along with recalling how the strikingly gorgeous Patricia had ogled Keiran.

Desiree yanked from his grip. "I think this is about a lot more than carpentry."

Neither of them broke the loaded silence as they advanced toward the cake display.

"She's trouble," Keiran said. "Supposedly, she helped me when I was building my carpentry business."

They'd come to the edge of the awning. Desiree leaned against a makeshift pole and crossed her arms. "Supposedly?"

"Aye. We rented an office together. She answered phone calls from customers, scheduled my jobs, and advertised my business. And, I trusted her with all the bookkeeping duties. Now that I look back, though, there were several times that I suspected money was missing."

"Did you confront her?"

"Are you kidding? Of course, although her answer was always the same. She'd nearly bite my head off and her resultant tantrum would last for days."

Desiree glanced at Teddy and Candee near the judges' stand. Teddy had his arm around Candee, and they chatted amiably with Rob.

Oh, to be able to give her heart to a man she could trust, Desiree thought, a man who loved her unconditionally.

She studied Keiran. "And that was okay with you?"

"Unfortunately, aye. I thought she was a prize—pretty, well-heeled, efficient. And then, she cheated on me with Kyle, a moneyed stockbroker."

The tension in the cold air between them crackled.

"You never told me any of this."

"I should have," he admitted. "Except it's demoralizing for a guy to have his girlfriend cheat on him with his best friend. They became a couple and—"

"And you skipped town to land on my doorstep."

"Patricia and I had a rocky relationship from the start. It's odd. Once the truth hit me, I realized I wanted the happily-ever-after ending. Just not with her."

"And yet, you couldn't bring yourself to tell me these revelations."

"I'm sorry. I should have." For a moment, he closed his eyes and breathed aloud. "Teddy said the same thing."

"You told Teddy, yet you wouldn't confide in me?" The surprise that had seized her when she'd realized who Patricia was to Keiran evaporated, along with the belief he actually cared. In a blinding flare of realization, she tore from his hold. "I'm a good listener, I would have understood. Now . . ."

"Nothing's changed."

The lump in her throat was so thick she could hardly manage any words. "Everything's changed."

"Because you're judgmental?"

"You're blaming me?" To stop from splintering into a million pieces, she shielded herself by opposing him. "You're the one who lied by omission."

"I couldn't admit it, okay? I thought I cared about a woman who was nothing more than a liar and a cheat. And then I realized I never cared at all, but wasn't sure how to make a proper exit."

"So your pride got in the way of your decision-making."

"Look, can I show you the silk scarf I saw earlier?" His jaw set with determination. "I think you'll like it."

"Please tell me you're joking."

"I'm completely serious." He laid his hands over hers. "We've got something good, Desiree. Surely you realize it too."

He didn't understand. He never could, considering his silver-spoon background. She'd been hurt and disappointed her entire life.

She winced. The only way to protect herself was to stay

away from precarious situations—the risk of heartache was too great.

"You don't get it," she said. "You weren't there when Candee and I were growing up. You didn't live where we lived."

A look of persistence passed across his features. "True, but I'm not to blame."

Angrily, she swiped at a tear running down her cheek.

"This isn't about me." He kept hold of her hands. "Or Patricia. It's about you growing up in the foster care system. You're afraid to open your heart because you might get hurt again. You can trust me, Desiree. I made a mistake and I'm genuinely sorry." He took her in his arms, lovingly stroking her hair. "Let's discuss this in a quiet place. We can have lunch at the new Chinese restaurant near my pub, and designate the occasion as our first real date."

"A date? *Now* we're dating?" Methodically, she removed his hands as Patricia headed toward them with sheer determination planted on her porcelain features.

"I'm back, Keiran," Patricia said, plunking dainty hands on her nonexistent hips while she perused the village green. "Where do you suggest we eat in this single-traffic-light town before we drive back to Atlanta together?"

"How about Chinese?" Desiree indicated the street where the restaurant was located. "It's across from the pub."

Keiran regarded Desiree levelly. "I'm buying you a silk scarf, and then I'm treating you to lunch to celebrate your cake victory."

"I've lost my appetite for eggrolls." Desiree cut her gaze to Patricia. "Although you'll love the food. Try the fried rice too. I've heard it's the best in Roses."

"I will, as long as he's buying. He's a generous guy." Patricia's thin eyebrows lifted in amused mockery. "Keiran, we can visit our pub too." Possessively, she touched his sleeve and beamed up at him.

"Desiree, please listen to me." He edged away from Patricia. "I can make everything right between us."

"You can't," Desiree shot back.

Her retort reverberated in her mind.

Or could he? They'd grown so close that they'd even begun finishing each other's sentences. One emotion bombarded her—hope—but hope would leave her brokenhearted if it didn't work out.

No. She couldn't take the chance.

"Enjoy your lunch, Keiran." For a second, Desiree forced herself to look at him. So handsome, so striking, so utterly appealing—and she faltered.

And then she reminded herself she wouldn't allow any more disappointment into her life. "We're done here," she said.

He met her look. "Really? You won't hear me out?"

She shook her head.

His green-eyed gaze froze to solid ice.

She twisted, trying not to recall the times in his arms, the pleasurable, passionate thrill of his kisses. Blindly, she made her way to the judges' stand, feeling the keenly inquisitive stares of strangers.

"We're not finished. I'll see you as soon as I get things sorted," he called out to her. "Back at the house. Wait for me there."

Drowning in sadness she couldn't control, she struggled to keep her shoulders straight and her gait sure. All around her, cheerful festivities rang out. The boutiques were filled to capacity. Shoppers spilled into the streets, and light-hearted conversation abounded.

"There you are." Candee raced through the throng and hauled Desiree to the side. "Teddy and I want to invite you and Keiran to our house for lunch. By the way, where is Keiran?" She peered around Desiree, shaded her eyes, and scowled. "Who is that woman he's walking with? I've never seen her before. Does she live in Roses?"

"She's from Atlanta."

"Why is she here?"

Why, indeed.

Desiree didn't answer her sister's question, although she agreed to lunch. The trembling that had started in her arms had spread to her legs, and later, she couldn't remember how she managed to get to her car, bypassing the green grocer as she drove home.

One fact she knew for sure. She wouldn't be waiting when Keiran arrived at her house. She couldn't bear the thought of facing him, yet she didn't have the prerogative to confront him. They weren't engaged or even officially dating, unless one counted nightly home-cooked meals as dates.

Sure, she'd presumed he'd told her the truth about his life in Atlanta, but he'd omitted a key point. He'd been seriously dating Patricia.

What did a lie by omission mean? Her lawyer brain clicked into gear. *Leaving out an important fact, thus fostering a misconception,* she automatically supplied. Yes, that described it.

As soon as she arrived home, she dashed off a note telling him to pack his things and leave, and set the note on her kitchen table. Then she planned to stay at Candee's house until midnight. Or longer, if Desiree saw his truck parked in her driveway.

CHAPTER 8

Desiree needn't have worried, because Keiran came and went while she lunched and spent the afternoon with Candee, Teddy, and Joseph.

Keiran had penned his own note and placed it on the kitchen table next to hers, explaining he was driving back to Atlanta with Patricia.

Not sure when I'll return. Will keep you posted, he'd written in his typical bold script.

She crumpled up his note and tossed it on the floor.

A dire, stabbing ache grew as she climbed the stairs to the attic apartment. Hesitating, she slowly opened the door and stared at the room in silence. His bed was neatly made. His scent pervaded the space—raw wood and the outdoors, a hint of sawdust and pine. All related to his job.

And his belongings had vanished.

She inhaled and leaned weakly against the door. Here it was, a week before Christmas, and he'd abandoned her to be with his former girlfriend. For all Desiree knew, Keiran and Patricia planned to return to Roses and renovate O'Malley's as a team.

Her feverish brain refused to accept that scenario, and she seriously considered moving out of her beloved town if that ever occurred. In comparison to Patricia, Desiree felt like an adolescent girl again—ordinary and inexperienced.

Goodbye Keiran, she thought, coming to terms with the fact that they'd gone in opposite directions.

After arriving in Atlanta, he texted and phoned numerous times.

She replied with a brief text: *Don't contact me. No texts, no calls, okay?*

A date when I return? he immediately countered. *It's Christmas, after all.*

And Christmas brought memories of when she was a little kid, feeling alone and deserted while her parents lay drunk on the living room couch. She knew she must come to grips with her emotions in order to move forward. But, oh, this was so hard. Acceptance and forgetting, these were weaknesses in her life she had a hard time acknowledging, although her favorite pastor had assured in a sermon that weakness led to strength.

When, exactly? Had God brought her a Christmas miracle in Keiran? And if so, was she throwing that miracle away with both hands when she refused to speak with him, allowing pride to dictate her lonely path?

She pressed her cell phone to her heart and asked the empty room, "How can I fight you, Keiran, when I'm warring with myself?"

The sparks between them had flamed with his every touch, his every kiss, and she missed his solid strength, calm reassurances, and good humor.

With a deep sigh, she tried to come to terms with the desolation weighing her down. How could she face another day without him when he made her feel so complete? Finally, she'd had a chance to be happy.

But happiness was a funny thing. The fear of being alone stemmed from her childhood, and she'd proven she could succeed on her own.

She reminded herself of all she'd accomplished, that her colleagues had remarked on her spirited, confident nature. With firm determination, she lifted her chin and pushed her thoughts of Keiran aside.

And then she texted him back. A final, single word: *No*.

By Monday of the following week, she knew he'd departed for good. Still, her heart jumped whenever the doorbell rang. Despite her firm reprimands to herself, she'd hurry to the front door, thinking he'd returned for Christmas after all. A secret fantasy come true, despite her conflicting emotions.

Although the opposite prevailed in her real world, and it turned out to be the postman, or an online store delivery.

Very well, then. The next time the doorbell rang, she would take her time answering it.

By the end of the week, she'd established a pattern. No longer did she live in suspended anticipation that Keiran might stride into her foyer. Nonetheless, neither was she able to anticipate the upcoming holiday with delight. She'd thought she'd find the peace she'd been looking for if she bought her own home.

But she hadn't.

Peace had little to do with the most expensive home, the most beautiful neighborhood, she decided. It was who you shared your home with that mattered most. And now that Keiran was gone, despite her attempts to deny it, the truth hit hard.

At six o'clock on the Friday evening before Christmas Eve, Desiree pulled off her black leather boots, hung her jacket in the hall closet, and pulled her blue cardigan over her silk blouse. She was done working for two weeks, and had won a case involving Julie Wallis, a single mother of two children, who was being jailed and fined for a minor offense. When it was clear the mother couldn't afford to pay, Desiree had argued for another solution. The court had accepted a community service plan, and Julie had cried with relief when she was released.

Cause for celebration, Desiree thought, although the day didn't feel at all celebratory.

It felt empty.

Aimlessly, she wandered the spacious rooms of her home, fingering the prominent wooden staircase, the paneled oak walls, the built-in china cabinets.

She barely glanced at her wristwatch as she stepped across the spacious foyer, although her mouth tightened when she realized the time. Candee was coming over in an hour to finalize their Christmas Eve plans.

As much as Desiree liked talking to Candee, she'd avoided her sister's phone calls because she'd been dreading their imminent discussion. Most likely, the topic would center around Keiran and his notable disappearance.

As Desiree headed for the kitchen, Candee phoned, launching into a lengthy monologue regarding the sweet rolls she was bringing for Christmas Eve dinner. Desiree cut her off, making an excuse that a thorough kitchen organization required her attention, and she'd see Candee at seven o'clock.

She poured herself a glass of sparkling cider, sat on a stool, and rehearsed their upcoming exchange in her mind.

"*What happened?*" Candee would ask, referring to Keiran. Most likely, she'd expected to find Desiree and Keiran acting like an official couple by the time Christmas rolled around.

"What happened?" Desiree would repeat. "Keiran lied to me, knowing I was falling in love with him. And then he went off with Patricia."

An unbearable ache pierced her heart. She set down her glass and perused the kitchen. A box of pots and pans required sorting, and her pantry could be more orderly.

As she arranged a variety of spices closer to the stove, a trio of deliverymen knocked on the kitchen's sliding glass doors. Her base cabinet had arrived, they announced, and her contractor had requested they bring the cabinet through the rear door rather than muddying up the new wood floors.

"Is the cabinet heavy?" She invited the men inside to unbox the cabinet in the earmarked corner near the pantry.

"Just awkward, ma'am," the youngest of the three replied, test-fitting the cabinet by what he clarified was dry-fitting. "Do you have a carpenter to install it?" he asked.

She shook her head.

"We're booked until the first of the year, but you're missing the stainless handle for this cabinet. If it's in stock, I'll make a note for a special delivery before Christmas."

"Thank you, and Merry Christmas," she replied.

As the men cheerfully departed, she bid them good-bye with a quiet smile.

She went into the pantry, intending to declutter the shelves by stacking the flat containers on top of one another. Instead, she found herself rummaging in a drawer to retrieve Keiran's note, which she'd salvaged from the floor.

Not sure when I'll return. Will keep you posted, he'd written.

Rereading the simple sentences, she traced the letters with shaking hands, feeling a pang of longing so intense, her knees weakened. He was so magnificent, so unbearably good-looking, she'd taken unabashed pleasure in spending every spare second with him.

If he phoned her even once more, she might cave and answer his call.

Might? Ruefully, she decided that she would answer.

Of course he hadn't, and her phone had sat silent for two days.

"I thought I had everything worked out," she whispered to the quiet pantry.

Apparently not this time. The storybook life she'd planned out hadn't gone the way she'd expected. And despite reaching her goals—her successful career and a home of her own—happiness remained elusive.

Pivoting, she walked into the living room, taking heart in its remarkable transformation, the Christmas tree illuminated in dazzling splendor. She lit a fire in the fireplace, and the flickering light assured her of comfort through the bitter winter ahead.

All week since Keiran's departure, she hadn't allowed herself to cry, and had accomplished her workdays briskly and efficiently. However, now that she didn't have court cases and clients to occupy her mind, the heavy burden of keeping her feelings bottled up threatened to spill over.

As tears welled, she shuffled back to the kitchen. The wintry December wind whistled through a small opening in the sliding glass doors and burned her eyes. She slid the doors closed as tears streamed freely down her cheeks.

She let them come, weeping until there were no tears left to shed—no more sadness or resentment. The picture in her mind's eye of where she was supposed to live, where the man in her life was supposed to stand, and the children she would be blessed with hadn't happened.

She sank onto a chair, her shoulders drooping with desolation. Why had Keiran refrained from telling her about Patricia? And why hadn't he returned to Roses by now? He'd given up so quickly. Wasn't he interested in knowing how Desiree was faring after their break-up?

Her thoughts went back to the previous weekend, and she

visualized Patricia's seductive eyes as she'd gazed intimately up at Keiran.

We were practically engaged, Patricia had said, her words intended to pierce.

Hurt, confused, and angry, Desiree refused to allow that image to dominate her thoughts. Instead, she recalled how Keiran had held her afterwards, murmuring to her, caressing her hair.

You can trust me, Desiree. I made a mistake and I'm genuinely sorry. His voice had been rough with self-reproach.

And later, the guarded hope in his tone as he'd called out, *I'll see you as soon as I get things sorted. Back at the house. Wait for me there.*

A stinging pain punctured her chest with each memory. He'd sounded sincere, and she remembered the despair that had crossed his handsome features.

She half-rose from her chair as a thought struck her. With surprising clarity, she recognized that the pain she felt was more for Keiran than herself.

Angrily, she swiped her wet cheeks and sprang fully to her feet. Surely this proved she was a besotted fool. How could she feel sorry for him when she was the person who'd been deceived?

Surprisingly, with that realization, her mood began to elevate. In fact, by the time she stood by the table and itemized her to-do list for Christmas Eve, she felt better than she had all week. Her sadness began turning into fortitude.

She opened the refrigerator and brought out two bags of fresh cranberries she intended to frost with sugar for a festive centerpiece. She'd also purchased a variety of prepared side dishes including creamy mashed potatoes and a green bean casserole topped with pecans. In the morning, she'd tackle the fresh turkey preparation.

So, the meal was set, and she'd slated her pistachio cake for dessert.

Her gaze travelled to the adjoining dining room.

Where would they all sit—Teddy, Candee, Joseph, and Desiree?

She paused, considered the lack of furniture, then recalled her conversation with Keiran.

You own a service of fine crystal and china, your dining area is large enough for a twenty-people feast, and there's no place to sit and enjoy a meal? he'd teased.

I'll pile cushions on the floor and we'll sit cross-legged, she'd replied.

Dashing back into the living room, she dragged her coffee table into the dining area. Then she draped a red tartan tablecloth over it and arranged colorful throw pillows around the table.

With great care, she set the table with four place settings using her finest china and silver, embellishing the tablespace with shiny silver candle holders and a string of sparkling white lights.

Pleased with the result, she went into the kitchen and sat in the middle of the tiled floor, eyeing the base cabinet waiting to be anchored.

The deliveryman had stated she needed a carpenter. Well, Keiran wasn't here.

However, she was.

On her phone, she searched tutorials on how to install a cabinet, and selected a step-by-step video that assured installation was easy with the proper tools, which included a level, a screw gun, screws, clamps, and a hammer and nails.

"Carefully measure and draw the exact location," the woman in the video instructed. "Drive screws into the wall studs to anchor the cabinet."

Quickly, Desiree changed into jeans and a sweatshirt,

chose the necessary tools from the study where the crewmen kept their supplies, and set to work.

An hour later, she was kneeling on the floor, concentrating intensely on the installation, when Candee entered the kitchen.

"Sorry I'm late," Candee declared as Desiree jerked back, startled by her sister's voice. "Boomer was doing his favorite thing—eating—and then I took him for a quick walk. You didn't hear the doorbell, so I let myself in." Candee's mouth trembled with laughter as she admired the cabinet. "And now I see why. You look remarkably determined."

"Base cabinets aren't difficult to install if the area has been measured accurately and you have the correct tools," Desiree said, parroting the singsong tone of the woman in the video. She finished driving the last nail into the toe kick beneath the cabinet, set the tools on the floor, then stood.

"Bravo!" Candee gave her a high-five. "The place looks great."

She smiled. "Thanks."

"Have you eaten dinner?" Candee's gaze skimmed the kitchen.

"No, and I'm starving." Desiree reminded herself that she needed to set aside a half hour a day for exercise in order to shed the extra ten pounds she'd gained. Appreciating Keiran's magnificent cooking, she hadn't had the opportunity or the inclination to diet.

"Teddy and I are so busy with Joseph and his horse therapy that I haven't eaten, either." Candee peered into the refrigerator and extracted cold cuts and bread, motioning for Desiree to join her. "I'll make us both a sandwich and brew a pot of tea."

The women enjoyed a cozy light supper at the kitchen table.

"You seem much better than I imagined," Candee said as she poured tea. "I mean, after last Saturday."

"I feel better."

"Care to fill me in on what happened between you and Keiran?" Candee fixed Desiree a mug of tea without milk, and added milk and sugar to her own. "Teddy mentioned he and Keiran have been in touch, but when I pressed him for details he was extremely close-lipped."

Desiree debated, opening her mouth to defend her position, then closing it. Today, for the first time in a week, she'd begun to feel purposeful again. A delicate newfound serenity had emerged through her tears. Should she take the risk of talking about it?

But Candee seemed so resolute, Desiree knew holding back was futile. Besides, who was better to confide in than her dear sister?

"Ask away," Desiree said.

"Tell me everything."

"Well," Desiree sat back in her chair, "I suppose our relationship began when he first arrived and began talking to my front porch."

"You mean talking *to you* on your front porch."

"No, I mean talking *to* my front porch," Desiree said with an amused smile. She couldn't explain her attraction to Keiran from that first moment. At night her dreams had been of him. During the day, she'd daydreamed about him. His capable hands as he cooked, or his bass voice as he sang an Irish tune, had awakened her desire for a secure, centered life with the man she loved. Often in the past weeks, she'd told herself that the uniqueness, the unqualified novelty, of having a charismatic Renaissance man living in her house would pass.

Instead, her feelings had intensified.

Noting Candee's raised eyebrows, Desiree set aside her

teacup. "When Keiran arrived, I told him I needed an electrician, not a carpenter, and to return in the morning. So I shut the door on him and when I reopened it, he was still there, muttering to the porch. I invited him to move into the attic because he had nowhere else to stay."

Candee laughed softly. "And then the relationship began."

"A practical relationship."

"A romantic one."

"At night after dinner, we'd go into the living room and he'd light a fire." Desiree drew her legs up in the chair, curling her arms around them. "He'd play his guitar and . . ."

When she finished her story, Candee dabbed at her eyes. "Truly, your entire courtship is enchanting."

"We've never even been out on a formal date."

"In all those hours you spent together you probably know him better than anyone. Teddy said that just because Keiran moved into your house didn't mean a relationship would develop, especially in a short period of time." A satisfied smile wreathed Candee's face. "But I felt certain he was wrong. I heard Keiran talk endlessly about you whenever he came to the house to confer with Teddy. And I watched you two at the cake judging contest, and I knew. He's deeply in love with you."

Desiree stood and wiped her palms on the folds of her sweatshirt. "He has an odd way of showing it, running off to Atlanta with Patricia."

"Has he tried contacting you?"

"He's called and texted many times."

"Have you responded?"

Desiree stared impassively at the glossy white backsplash above the farmhouse sink Keiran had installed. "Only to tell him not to contact me again."

"Well, that's a brilliant way to go about things."

Desiree gave a guilty start. Her heartbeat raced with a

surge of annoyance. Or was it culpability?

Candee crossed the room and took Desiree's cold hands in hers. "Do you love him?"

Understatement. Sweet memories hastened to her mind. With a rush of happiness, she recalled his attentiveness, his patience, the pride she'd felt when he complimented her for fighting court battles against injustice. This broad-shouldered, rugged man gazed at her with such heartfelt tenderness, sometimes words would lodge in her throat.

"Did you think about me today?" he'd asked.

"Often."

"Good. I thought about you too. See how much we are alike? We both love Christmas and we both love—" Then he'd drawn her into his arms and kissed her.

Desiree willed herself to say no, she didn't love him. Instead, she heard herself saying, "Yes. I fell in love with him at a high school football game ten years ago."

Candee tightened her grip on Desiree's hands. "I thought I recognized his name when Teddy first brought him up. Then O'Malley's pub was discussed and I recalled you going on and on about him when we were teenagers. So often, in fact, I suspected you had a crush on him."

"You were right," Desiree said. "But now I'm a grown woman."

"Who loves a grown man. And that man loves you very much."

Desiree shook free and peered out the window at the thick dark night, chilly and moonless.

"He's gone," she said quietly.

"He's not gone." Candee went to the sink and ran soapy hot water over a stack of dishes. "He's just waiting for you to give him the opportunity to make amends. You can't repair a relationship if you avoid him."

"He hasn't texted or called in a couple of days."

"He's probably come to accept that you don't want anything to do with him."

"That's not true."

"Then go to him in Atlanta. And tell him face to face."

Desiree's brain frantically groped for a way to refute Candee's argument. Suppose she failed? He was obviously more interested in Patricia.

"I can't. Tomorrow is Christmas Eve. We're attending church service, and I'm cooking. See?" Desiree gestured to the dining room. "The table's all set."

"Then I'll give you a one-day pass because you admitted you love him."

Her love for him was out of reach, but she knew if she admitted her thoughts to Candee, her sister would argue her point a tad too vehemently.

"Yes, I love him," Desiree said. Desperately loved him. And when he gazed at her as if she were the only person in his universe, her pulse surged with excitement.

"Settled. On Christmas Day, you're driving to Atlanta," Candee said. "Teddy knows where Keiran used to live, and you'll start there. Or, you can phone him."

Desiree hesitated. Would Keiran be angry with her, or coolly polite? Or would he be thrilled to see her, because he still cared?

Desiree blew out a breath. "I'll surprise him."

Although, as she closed the door after Candee's departure, she felt a sickening fear of failure straight to her belly.

Suppose she interrupted Keiran while he was with Patricia?

Suppose he didn't want to see her?

With resolve, she pulled her thoughts away from irrational worry and concentrated on their reunion in Atlanta.

Please love me, my affectionate, gentle Renaissance man, she thought, *as much as I love you.*

CHAPTER 9

Keiran didn't return to Roses in two days, which was the time frame he'd originally planned. Neither did he spend his days with Patricia.

He'd passed on lunching with her in Roses, and hadn't taken her inside O'Malley's. He'd left her in town, driven back to Desiree's home, and read her note with surprised alarm. She wouldn't hear him out.

He'd been raised a gentleman, and quickly packed his bags as she requested and loaded up his truck. It didn't matter who was right or wrong. He'd kept the truth from her, although not intentionally. He'd simply removed Patricia from his heart and mind because Desiree had taken over his thoughts. When he was with her, everything else fell away.

After a silent four-hour drive with Patricia back to Atlanta, he'd dropped her at her apartment. He intended to get to the bottom of her demands, settle any financial score once and for all, and return to Roses, his true home.

And his true love, Desiree.

When Desiree hadn't answered his phone calls or texts in

the ensuing first hours of his departure, he'd tasted a bitter defeat. But not for long. They weren't finished by a long shot.

He bunked in his former apartment, where he discussed his situation with Oscar and Georges. Oscar made a hasty phone call and booked a consultation with Abraham Realgood, Honest Abe, the lawyer he worked for. Although the lawyer wasn't accepting new clients, he'd offer his consultation services as a favor to Oscar.

The following afternoon, Mr. Realgood's receptionist showed Keiran into a dark-paneled office where the lawyer greeted Keiran with a friendly tilt of his head.

"What can I do for you?" He gestured for Keiran to take a seat across from him.

"I'll come directly to the point." Keiran sank into the cushioned chair. "My former girlfriend, Patricia, believes she's entitled to half my earnings, including a pub I inherited."

A pair of astute hazel eyes measured Keiran. "I've heard some of your story, thanks to Oscar and Georges."

"Then can you advise me? I want Patricia out of my life."

"She's requesting money."

"Yes, and more money than I have." With Patricia, it had always been about an extravagant lifestyle, and when she had a goal in mind there was no stopping her.

"Is she entitled to your money?" the lawyer asked.

"When we were together, we had a verbal agreement that we would split half my earnings. I did the work, and she maintained the office and books. However, I've reviewed the paperwork I held on to, because she implied there was some fine print," Keiran said. "I couldn't find anything written down."

"How much does she want?"

"Twenty thousand dollars. I wish it was less. She found out I inherited a pub and she wants me to sell it and she'll take half the proceeds. However, I'm not willing to sell, and besides, the building isn't worth much in its present condition."

"Not functioning?"

"It hasn't been open in many years."

"Is there a possibility she'd take you to court?"

That was a worrisome and infuriating thought. Keiran stretched out his long legs and blew out a sigh. "Knowing Patricia? Aye, although she couldn't possibly win. Could she?"

"Probably not, if your agreement was verbal, but this battle could go on for years. It all depends how badly you want her out of your life."

Furious with himself for getting involved with her in the first place, Keiran glanced out the window at the overcast sky. "I'd like our relationship to be finished, once and for all."

"Then there's a solution because money talks." The lawyer examined the paperwork on his desk and idly pushed it to the side. "Georges mentioned you inherited an autographed football card that might be valuable."

With a nod, Keiran pulled the card from its protective case, as Georges had urged him to bring it to the meeting. He felt a deep, almost agonizing sadness about giving up the card that had meant so much to his father. He'd prayed about it, and realized he needed to get over the sadness and guilt if he sold it. If he reopened the pub, his parents would undoubtedly be grateful and proud. As much as his father's dream had been football, the pub in Roses was his legacy.

Keiran shifted his gaze to the lawyer's sparsely furnished, dimly lit office. He'd expected an oily charmer with a law degree, but Abraham Realgood seemed on the up and up.

"We appraised the card at the pawn shop Georges works for," Keiran said. "The estimate from the pawnbroker is fifteen thousand dollars."

Seemingly impervious to Keiran's emotional state, the lawyer grinned. "I advise you to sell the card and pay the ex. If your past agreement was verbal, you're in the clear, but it's more the matter of guaranteeing she won't be able to badger you for any more money. Otherwise, she may turn up again. More time. More money. Do you want that?"

Keiran shook his head. "I'd like her gone from my life."

"Then I'll draw up a contract, a full and final release stating clearly she's not entitled to anything else after this payment."

"Do you think she'll accept less than she's asking?"

Mr. Realgood rubbed his jaw. "From you and your friends' descriptions, I'm positive she'll jump at it. Fifteen thousand dollars is a lot, especially around Christmas."

"Excellent." It was all Keiran could do not to burst into an Irish song. This was going to work. "How soon can the contract be drafted?"

"By tomorrow. I'll handle everything from here." Slowly, the gray-haired lawyer leaned back in his chair and folded his hands behind his head. "Now I'm not judging, mind you, but if I were you I'd avoid any further correspondence with your ex—verbal or otherwise."

The lawyer *was* judging, Keiran reflected, although he was too relieved to do anything other than watch Mr. Realgood write out a bill and hand it to him.

Keiran looked over the number and gaped.

"Admittedly, my services are costly on account of the short notice and holiday season," the lawyer said. "But your problem is solved. And if you ever need your locks changed, I'll cut you a good deal."

"Thank you." With a deep, relieved breath, Keiran shook hands with the lawyer and left.

By noon the next day, Abe Realgood phoned to report

that Patricia had received the email and accepted via her electronic signature.

Another deep breath of relief.

"The thing is," Keiran told a frowning but somewhat amused Georges and Oscar, "I can't stay to cook Christmas Eve dinner because I'm driving back to Roses."

Georges flashed Keiran a mischievous grin. "What will we eat then, *mon ami?*"

"Why don't you call the local pizzeria? They deliver on Christmas Eve, and pizza goes great with beer." Keiran chuckled as he hoisted his belongings over his shoulder, thanked the men for their help, and wished them a Merry Christmas.

He glanced at his watch. He had two stops to make in Roses, and one important phone call. He hoped he wouldn't be late for Christmas Eve dinner. They ate at six o'clock sharp.

* * *

"YOU BURNED THE TURKEY?" Candee hovered over Desiree, who'd dashed into the kitchen to extract a charred, smoking turkey from the oven. "How can anyone burn a fourteen-pound turkey?"

"Fortunately, it didn't catch fire. When the smoke detector went off, I was worried," Desiree replied. "I went into the living room for a few minutes to start a fire in the fireplace and plug in the Christmas tree lights. Then, while I was lighting the candles on the mantel, I got sidetracked when the radio started playing 'Silent Night' on repeat."

Desiree wore the red and green *Kiss Me, It's Christmas* apron over a red silk blouse and black velvet pants. Christmas Eve was a special occasion, and she planned to slip on suede ankle boots and her cobalt-blue wool coat for midnight church services. To keep her hair away from her face while cooking, she'd pinned it into a chignon secured with a red jeweled clasp.

"I should've helped you with the dinner preparations. Sorry I lost track of time. I love watching Teddy and Joseph play a game of flag football," Candee said. "It's amazing—we haven't gotten any snow this year so the guys are still wearing sweatshirts and jeans."

"The weather forecast predicts a light dusting by midnight." Desiree glanced out the kitchen window at the energetic twosome. They'd decided on another game and were flipping a coin. Then Teddy placed the football in the middle of her large backyard. Starting with a snap, Joseph passed the ball in one fluid motion to a third player.

"Recognize that handsome guy? He looks like he could be a male model." Candee feigned fanning herself as she came to stand by the window with Desiree.

He certainly seemed familiar, with his broad shoulders and midnight-black hair and . . .

Desiree's knees buckled. No, it couldn't be. The guy must be one of the neighborhood men, perhaps Mr. Juno taking a break from his graduate studies.

"I'll try flipping the turkey," Candee suggested. "If I drop it, then we can remember this Christmas as the year you burned the turkey and it fell to the floor."

Desiree laughed. "As long as it doesn't roll into the dining room and—"

The front doorbell rang. The cabinet door handle delivery man, Desiree surmised, because she wasn't expecting any visitors.

Or was she?

She told herself to take her time answering, but scratched the idea as she hastened to the door and swung it open.

It wasn't the delivery man.

He stood on her front porch, tall and lean, his green eyes reminding her of Irish emeralds glimmering in his handsome face. He wore his navy-blue parka, unzipped, accentuating his toned physique. His denim shirt and jeans were rumpled. He was holding a small gift, wrapped in brown paper and tied with a red satin ribbon.

"Keiran." She stepped back and attempted to breathe. Part of her functioning brain reminded her that she should stay calm and composed.

"Merry Christmas, Desiree." He held out the gift.

She kept her hands at her sides. "Why are you here?" Her voice shook. He still offered her the gift, his hands outstretched.

"To finish our discussion from last week. And to tell you what I've wanted to say since we met. Listen—"

"Keiran, you're a little late." Candee approached and gave him a mildly sardonic smile.

"It started to snow in Atlanta and the limited visibility on I-85 slowed traffic," he said. "Plus I stopped in town to buy Desiree's gift, then ducked into my pub. Rob is coming in the morning."

"Rob?" Desiree regarded them both. "Why?"

"Rob and Keiran are reopening the pub. Rob is loaning him the start-up money, much as he did for Teddy when he began his real estate flipping business," Candee said.

"Rob and I will be serving Christmas dinner tomorrow to the homeless in our community," Keiran explained. "Several of the markets in town, including your green grocer, are donating food. We're using the ovens at the local supermarkets to prepare the meals. I hope you'll join us, Desiree."

Blinking, Desiree gaped at Keiran, and then Candee. "And you knew about all this?"

"Only recently," Candee replied. "Teddy and Keiran arranged everything."

"And about Keiran returning here? Tonight?"

Feigning innocence, Candee gushed apologetically. "You wouldn't answer his texts. Tonight, Teddy told me they've been in touch all week. And now I'm going to see to dinner." Candee rolled up the sleeves of her glittery silver blouse and hurried away.

"Keiran." Desiree touched her throat. "I don't know what to say."

His strong fingers were gentle as he pressed them against her lips. "Take my gift and invite me inside."

"Please come in." She accepted his gift. "You didn't need to buy me anything. Thank you."

He stepped inside. "I confess I used the gift as an excuse."

"What? I don't understand."

"I've been working all week to make things right between us. I understand you're hurt and justifiably angry. I met with a lawyer in Atlanta, and Patricia signed a full and final release contract. She's not entitled to half of what I earn anymore. Our former business agreement was verbal, by the way."

Desiree's heart was pounding so hard, he could surely hear each beat. "What do you mean?"

"She was demanding twenty thousand dollars, the estimated proceeds if I sold the pub." He shook his head. "You don't know her the way I do. She would have made our lives miserable. So, I gave her fifteen thousand, and made certain she's out of our life for good."

Desiree's gaze narrowed. "Where did you get the money? Rob?"

"Rob's been great, but no."

She paused for a beat. "Then where?"

"My father's football card. I didn't want to sell it, and I prayed long and hard before agreeing. The pawn shop assured me they'll hold it for a while, in case I can come up with the money to buy it back. I don't see that happening, but you never know. Our pub might become extremely successful, just like it once was."

"*Our* pub?"

"I'm hoping you'll help me bring it back to its former glory."

Through tears of happiness, she found her voice. "With you at the helm, how can it fail?"

"And you," he said solemnly. "I hope I'm the man you deserve, and I want to make all my mistakes up to you."

The pain in his voice brought a new swell of tears. "Keiran, please, we all make mistakes and—"

"I'm sorry, Desiree. And I love you."

When she realized he was threading his fingers through her hair, then cupping her face so he could kiss her, she whispered the words bursting from her heart. "I love you too."

All week she'd dreamed of kissing him—the tenderness of his mouth on hers, the elation of being reunited. For a long moment, she felt mesmerized, like she was floating. His kiss was light and sweet, and magnificently poignant.

She snuggled against his warm, hard chest, feeling the solid beat of his heart. There was so much she wanted to tell him—that she'd installed a kitchen cabinet by herself, that she'd won a particularly difficult court case.

Not knowing where to begin, she burst out, "I burned the turkey. But I set a lovely table for dinner and I wasn't going to let a little thing like charred meat stop us from enjoying Christmas."

He chuckled. "Let me survey the damage and see if I can help." He removed his parka and Desiree hung it in the front foyer closet, then placed his gift on a side table in the living room. She crossed to the kitchen, where Keiran was deftly removing the burnt skin from the turkey.

"If everyone likes the legs and thighs, we're golden," he said.

Desiree set out her turkey platter, and Candee artfully arranged sliced lemons and sprigs of rosemary around the carved meat Keiran placed on the platter. He asked Desiree to stir the gravy on the stove.

"You're a little bossy."

His eyes crinkled as a grin touched his lips. "I'm delegating."

Teddy and Joseph joined the group, and they settled, cross-legged, on the cushions Desiree had arranged in the dining room around the makeshift table.

Dinner was a feast that did credit to all of Desiree's preparations. She glanced uncertainly at Keiran as he tasted a slice of turkey. He proclaimed the meat expertly roasted, and she couldn't help but notice he gazed at her with profound pride.

She toyed with the mashed potatoes, wishing she hadn't felt so nervous about entertaining. Keiran assumed the role as host with a casual, gracious elegance.

After her pistachio cake was served for dessert, Joseph turned his attention to her. "We have a present for you, Aunt Desiree!" he burst out. "It's a surprise! Uncle Teddy said we could go back to our house and get him as soon as we were finished." He turned to Candee. "May I be excused?"

Him? Get *him*? Before Desiree could ask, Candee opened her mouth with the obvious intention of suggesting they wait until Christmas morning, but Teddy forestalled her by grinning at Joseph in agreement.

"This won't take long," Teddy said, as he and Joseph hurried out the door.

They returned ten minutes later holding Boomer, the brown and tan beagle pup.

"Merry Christmas, Desiree!" Candee, Teddy, and Joseph chimed.

The beagle wriggled out of Joseph's arms and lunged for the coffee table laden with food.

"This dog loves to eat, so he must think he's landed in paradise because he can reach the height of this table," Teddy said.

Desiree dissolved with laughter. Her contentment was so real, she thought her chest might burst. This was heaven—a happy home, sharing God's message of joy with the people she loved.

After the meal was cleared, Keiran escorted Desiree to the living room while Candee and her family excused themselves to go back to their house and get ready for church services.

Boomer, apparently full and exhausted, curled up near the fireplace, tail to nose.

"Desiree? There are a few things we need to discuss." Keiran claimed a seat beside her on the sofa. Although he asked gently, she knew by his inquisitive expression that he wanted an explanation for why she refused to accept his phone calls and texts.

She pulled off her apron and smoothed her red silk blouse. Drawing a long breath, she told him her feelings about trust, knowing he'd been correct in surmising her issues had come from early life experiences.

"Trust can be relearned," he said quietly. "It helps if you talk about it. And I'll be here for you, to listen."

"You're moving back in?"

He brushed a wisp of blond hair from her face. "I hope you'll invite me to sleep in your attic. I can't drive back to Atlanta in a blizzard."

"I wouldn't call a few inches of snow a blizzard." She stared out the wavy glass of the front bay window. The snow was starting to fall, its thick wet flakes covering the sidewalks and road in a white blanket.

"You don't want your fiancé to be homeless," he said.

"Fiancé?"

Although his tone was light, she heard the rough tinge in his voice.

Tipping her chin up, he gazed deeply into her eyes. "I love you, Desiree."

She laid a hand on his cheek. "And I love you."

Her Renaissance man. She attempted to smile. "Until now, I felt certain I'd never hear those words from you."

"Desiree, I've loved you since you slammed the door in my face when I first arrived, then berated me for talking to your front porch."

"A bit odd, don't you think? Talking to a porch?"

"Not considering the circumstances." With an arm around her waist, he turned to a side table, picked up his gift and handed it to her.

"I thought about something Christmassy, and it's one of the reasons I stopped in town. Please open it."

She unwrapped the gift and slid a silky scarf between her fingers, admiring the holly design in white and green. "Thank you. It's gorgeous."

"The boutique owner said it's a designer scarf, and the colors will go with everything."

"Ideal for the holidays." She tied the scarf around her throat and smiled. "How does it look?"

"Perfect. Like you." He nodded to the box. "There's something else inside, at the bottom."

"What is it?"

He caught her in a long embrace. "Something special that I hope you'll love."

She unsnapped the lid of a tiny black velvet box and

gasped. An exquisite round-cut diamond ring, styled in yellow gold, reflected sparkling white light across the ceiling.

"I've never seen anything so beautiful," she breathed.

He drew back slightly and regarded her. "Will you marry me?"

From the moment he'd returned, Desiree had known he would ask for an open and honest relationship.

Through tears of bliss, she whispered, "Yes."

His arms closed around her. "Good. Because if you don't mean it, I won't bake any more Irish whiskey cakes."

"Maybe it's better, because I need to lose a few pounds." She laughed through her tears. "Besides, you never shared your secret recipe with me."

He took her hand and led her to the kitchen. "We can start this evening. I promise I'll teach you everything I know."

THE END

RECIPE FOR DESIREE'S PISTACHIO CAKE

Easy, fast, and festive, this recipe is always a treat!

You will need:

1 package of white cake mix- any brand

1 package of pistachio instant pudding – sugar-free may be used instead of regular

½ cup vegetable oil

½ cup water

½ cup milk

5 eggs

Blend cake mix with the package of pudding. Add oil, milk, and water. Add eggs one at a time, beating well with electric mixer after each addition.

Pour into a greased (or sprayed with cooking spray) tube or Bundt pan.

Bake 1 hour at 350 degrees. May be done sooner, as ovens vary.

Cool for 30 minutes, and invert onto favorite cake platter.

For a light and festive topping, sprinkle with sifted confectioners sugar and sliced maraschino cherries.

Optional frosting recipe: (Spread on cooled cake)

½ pint heavy cream

1 package instant pistachio pudding (sugar free may be used)

1 container thawed Cool Whip (fat-free may be used)

Beat heavy cream until thick. Blend in rest of ingredients. Frost as desired.

Enjoy!

A NOTE FROM JOSIE

Dear Friends,

Thank you for reading *1-800-CHRISTMAS,* the second book in my contemporary sweet romance series: *Flipping for You.*

If you loved this sweet romance as much as I loved writing it, please help other people find *1-800-CHRISTMAS* by posting your amazing review, as well as for the bundle: The 1-800-Series.

House flipping is a subject I've always been fascinated with. In my spare time, I enjoy watching home-improvement television shows, and several of these programs were an inspiration for my story.

1-800-CHRISTMAS continues the series in the same small town of Roses, North Carolina, and follows 1-800-CUPID.

Be sure to read the third book in the series, 1-800-IRELAND, which brings in 2 favorite characters from my previous sweet romances. Books 4, 5, and 6 in the 1-800-series are also available.

1-800-CHRISTMAS is available in ebook, paperback, Large Print Paperback, Hardcover, and audiobook.

I'd love to meet you in person someday, but in the meantime, all I can offer is a sincere and grateful thank you. Without your support, my books would not be possible.

As I write my next sweet or inspirational romance, remember this: Have you ever tried something you were afraid to try because it mattered so much to you? I did, when I started writing. Take the chance, and just do something you love.

With sincere appreciation,

Josie Riviera

ACKNOWLEDGMENTS

An appreciative thank you to my patient husband, Dave, and our three wonderful children.

ABOUT THE AUTHOR

Josie Riviera is a *USA TODAY* bestselling author of contemporary, inspirational, and historical sweet romances that read like Hallmark movies. She lives in the Charlotte, NC, area with her wonderfully supportive husband. They share their home with an adorable shih tzu, who constantly needs grooming, and live in an old house forever needing renovations.

Become a member of my Read and Review VIP Facebook group for exclusive giveaways and ARCs.

To connect with Josie, visit her webpage and subscribe to her newsletter. As a thank-you, she'll send you a free sweet romance novella directly to your inbox.

josieriviera.com

ALSO BY JOSIE RIVIERA

Seeking Patience

Seeking Catherine (always Free!)

Seeking Fortune

Seeking Charity

Seeking Rachel

The Seeking Series

Oh Danny Boy

I Love You More

A Snowy White Christmas

A Portuguese Christmas

Holiday Hearts Book Bundle Volume One

Holiday Hearts Book Bundle Volume Two

Holiday Hearts Book Bundle Volume Three

Holiday Hearts Book Bundle Volume Four

Candleglow and Mistletoe

Maeve (Perfect Match)

A Love Song To Cherish

A Christmas To Cherish

A Valentine To Cherish

A Christmas Puppy To Cherish

A Homecoming To Cherish

A Summer To Cherish

Romance Stories To Cherish

Romance Stories To Cherish Volume Two

Cherished Hearts Six Book Volume

Aloha To Love

Sweet Peppermint Kisses

Valentine Hearts Boxed Set

1-800-CUPID

1-800-CHRISTMAS

1-800-IRELAND

1-800-SUMMER

1-800-NEW YEAR

The 1-800-Series Sweet Contemporary Romance Bundle

Irish Hearts Sweet Romance Bundle

Holly's Gift

A Chocolate-Box Christmas

A Chocolate-Box New Years

A Chocolate-Box Valentine

A Chocolate-Box Summer Breeze

A Chocolate-Box Christmas Wish

A Chocolate-Box Irish Wedding

Chocolate-Box Hearts

Chocolate-Box Hearts Volume Two

Chocolate-Box Double Hearts

Recipes From The Heart

Leading Hearts

New Year Hearts

SENIOR HEARTS

Summer Hearts

Christmas in the Air (1-800-Book)

A Very Christian Christmas

Most books are available in ebook, audiobook, paperback, Large Print paperback and Hardcover.

Many are FREE on Kindle Unlimited!

1-800-CUPID (A SWEET CONTEMPORARY ROMANCE) PREVIEW

Chapter One

Twenty thousand dollars.

Click.

Candee Contando licked her dry lips. She'd done it. She'd placed an online bid on a home-auction website for the Victorian mansion on Thompson Lane. Her dream home, her dollhouse. Her dilapidated project.

Two years of savings. Gone.

No matter. Under her guidance, she'd transform the mansion to its former majestic state, painted a mustard-yellow offset by ornamental burnt-sienna "gingerbread" trim. The sounds of children's giggling and music and barking beagles—yes, beagles—would echo across all five acres of the property.

She surveyed her offer and beamed, savoring the moment.

Now if she only could ensure that no one else bid on the property and drove up the price.

She studied the ticking clock on the website. Stay optimistic, she told herself. Deteriorated by age and wear, the Victorian would scare off any prospective buyer.

She pushed away from her desk and surveyed her real estate office. Although only one room, she prided herself on the cheery décor. One wall featured photos of North Carolina—the majestic peaks of the Blue Ridge parkway and scenic waterfalls. Below the photos hung a map of the area with local real estate listings highlighted by pushpins.

She peered out the window into the street below. Since noon, a bright sun had been at odds with January's wind—a wind crazy in its intent to blow the streetlights off their wires.

For the umpteenth time, she checked her nonringing cell phone for messages. Surely the real estate market in Roses, North Carolina, would improve. Didn't prospective home buyers begin looking in January? And wouldn't these buyers call her rather than her competitors? Candee prided herself on her professionalism and up-to-date listings.

Then why hadn't she made a single sale since August?

On the heel of that depressing assessment came a cheerful one. In two hours, she and her older sister, Desiree, planned to enjoy dinner at Desiree's country club.

Candee stepped back to her desk and switched off the computer.

Two single women in their late twenties, she mused, spending Friday night alone and dateless, four weeks before Valentine's Day.

Her cell phone rang, most likely Desiree firming up dinner plans and reminding Candee not to be late. Regardless of what time Candee met her older sister anywhere, Desiree always arrived before her.

Candee clicked on her phone. "1-800-Cupid," she said with a laugh.

"Contando Realty?" a man asked.

"Yes, yes ..." So much for professionalism. Candee felt her cheeks color. She hurried to her desk, dropping into the chair and switching her phone to speaker. "Are you looking to buy a home today, sir?"

"I am." The man hesitated. "Is this the correct number?"

She powered on her computer. "Absolutely."

"I'm new to the area and checked into the Roses Hotel last night," he said.

Envisioning the rundown hotel, Candy raised her eyebrows. Although in all fairness, the hotel was the only lodging open in the winter. Roses, North Carolina, was a summer tourist town known for bubbling hot springs and cool mountain temperatures.

Her fingers poised on the keyboard. "I'm more than happy to assist. Your name?"

"Teddy. Teddy Winchester." He had a deep voice, a slight southern drawl.

"What type of home are you searching for, Mr. Winchester?"

"The worst home in the best neighborhood."

Yup. It figured. No significant sales commission to pay the mortgage this month. Fortunately, her part-time job at the local hardware store was stable, although the pay was meager.

She scrolled through the listings. "For yourself, sir?"

"I'm an investor."

"How many bedrooms and baths?"

"Three bedrooms, two baths. Single family and one level."

"Budget?"

"Anything below $50,000."

She rubbed the back of her neck. *Who did he think she was, a miracle worker?*

"Mr. Winchester, the nicer neighborhoods in Roses are priced well above $100,000."

"Nope. Too high."

Certainly a man of few words.

"Perhaps—"

"I'll take another look on the Internet." He seemed to ignore her completely. "Thanks anyway."

She wouldn't lose a potential sale.

"Wait." She feigned checking a non-existent schedule. "I may have an opening this afternoon. I know the area well and I'll find properties to show you. Will three o'clock work?"

"In a half hour? Fine. I admire a realtor who works fast. Should I meet you at your office? The address is listed on the Internet."

Candee verified the street number and ended the phone call with a cheery, "See you at three."

She clicked off and checked her watch. Thirty minutes wasn't enough time to drive to her apartment and change. Her worn jeans and blue flannel shirt would have to suffice.

Immediately, she phoned Desiree. "I may be late for dinner."

"I'm so glad it's you," Desiree said. "Scott, a new lawyer at the firm, asked me out tonight. Barring the fact the invitation was last minute, I said yes. Desperation, right?" She paused. "Can we plan for dinner together tomorrow night instead?"

"Right, sure. The reason I called is because I have a client who's interested in seeing some properties."

"You have a real live client?" Desiree cut immediately to the question.

Candee envisioned her sister, thick blonde hair piled high, sitting behind a mahogany desk in her law firm. Proper, well-dressed, every inch the high-powered attorney. Desiree had proven that, with the right help, a disadvantaged childhood could lead to a successful adulthood. She worked late hours at her law firm advocating justice for low-income families and their children.

"He's an investor," Candee said.

"Maybe he's tall, dark, and handsome?" Desiree said with deceptive casualness. "And rich?"

"Investors are usually short bald men." Candee adjusted her shirt's wrinkled collar, then checked out the frayed hem of her jeans. She let out a frustrated groan and ran a hand through her unruly auburn waves.

"You'll need a rich man if you plan to go through with your insane idea to purchase that Victorian," Desiree said. "The place will eat up all the money you hope to earn in a lifetime."

"I'll handle most of the work myself. Remember, when we lived in foster care, I learned carpentry from the family who took us in."

"How will you offer a quality after-school environment to disadvantaged kids if you're busy driving nails into crumbling walls?"

"Watch me." Briefly, Candee squeezed her eyes shut. It was her turn to pay it forward.

"Well, don't discount short men. They prefer tall, willowy red-heads with green eyes," Desiree said. "Who knows? He might be struck by Cupid's golden arrow when he meets you. This guy might be the one."

Candee drew in a breath. "The one what, exactly?"

"Your partner, your love, your support system. The one who can help pay off the mountainous amount of debt you'll incur if you actually buy the biggest dilapidated disaster in the state."

"Someone supportive? For me? After what happened?"

*** End of Excerpt *1-800-CUPID* by Josie Riviera ***

Read the rest of Candee's story.

Snag your copy of 1-800-CUPID today! FREE on Kindle Unlimited.

A house flipper looking for quick profit. A survivor with a dream. Can two broken hearts find a place to call home?

Made in the USA
Middletown, DE
30 April 2023